What the crit

5 stars! "*Ms. Havlir* creates such a sensually delicious romance in *Bodyguard* that all I could do was strap-in and hold on for dear life. Thank you, *Ms. Havlir,* for creating a hot cop story that delights all the senses!" ~ *Keely Skillman, EcataRomance Reviews*

"*Beverly Havlir* sets off at a pace that will have readers glued to every page with her well thought out suspenseful plot and fully defined strong, sensual characters." ~ *Tracy Marsac, Romance Junkies*

"*Bodyguard* sizzles with intensity and chemistry from beginning to end." ~ *Jennifer Bishop, Romance Reviews Today.*

"This story will keep the reader glued to the page. It is extremely hard to put down. Detective Nick Santorelli is one of the sexiest heroes I have come across in a long time. I would love to have him as my bodyguard." ~ *Candy, Coffee Time Romance*

"A definite 'keeper'." ~ *Mireya Orsini, Just Erotic Romance Reviews*

"Bodyguard is an utterly enjoyable book that will keep the reader turning the pages. The sex scenes are scorching." ~ *Luisa, Cupid's Library Reviews*

BEVERLY HAVLIR

*Body*GUARD

An Ellora's Cave Romantica Publication

www.ellorascave.com

Bodyguard

ISBN # 1419952757

Edited by: Heather Osborn
Cover art by: Syneca

Electronic book Publication: April, 2005
Trade paperback Publication: October, 2005

Warning:

The following material contains graphic sexual content meant for mature readers. *Bodyguard* has been rated *E-rotic* by a minimum of three independent reviewers.

Ellora's Cave Publishing offers three levels of Romantica™ reading entertainment: S (S-ensuous), E (E-rotic), and X (X-treme).

S-e*nsuous* love scenes are explicit and leave nothing to the imagination.

E-*rotic* love scenes are explicit, leave nothing to the imagination, and are high in volume per the overall word count. In addition, some E-rated titles might contain fantasy material that some readers find objectionable, such as bondage, submission, same sex encounters, forced seductions, etc. E-rated titles are the most graphic titles we carry; it is common, for instance, for an author to use words such as "fucking", "cock", "pussy", etc., within their work of literature.

X-*treme* titles differ from E-rated titles only in plot premise and storyline execution. Unlike E-rated titles, stories designated with the letter X tend to contain controversial subject matter not for the faint of heart.

Also by Beverly Havlir:

The Abduction of Emma

Taming Alex

Bodyguard

Dedication:

For Jim

Thanks for the love, support and inspiration.
This wouldn't be possible without you.

Trademarks Acknowledgement

The author acknowledges the trademarked status and trademark owners of the following wordmarks mentioned in this work of fiction:

Tums: SmithKline Beecham
Mensa: American Mensa Limited
Jeep: DaimlerChrysler
Scrabble: Hasbro, Inc.
Porsche: Dr. Ing. H.C.F. Porsche K.G. Company

Prologue

Life was good. Paige Harrington smiled as she headed up to the third level of the mall parking structure. Her arms were laden with shopping bags full of new clothes. Change was a good thing, and the new Paige was about to emerge.

Independence had set her free from her cocoon.

She grinned. It had taken her a long time to convince her father to let her move in to her own apartment. Not that she blamed him. Paige knew it was because she was an only child and he'd cosseted her all her life. But Daddy had to accept that she was a grown woman now. She had her own life to live.

Out with the old Paige, and in with the new.

Giddy with her newfound freedom, she'd even bought a new car after she acquired her driver's license recently, a nifty little Porsche that set her back a good amount. Oh, but it was a dream to drive. She relished the feeling of being able to go wherever she wanted without relying on chauffeurs or cabs.

The next step would be to get a boyfriend.

Paige flushed. She was way behind on that one, but she planned on making up for lost time. Oh, if her father knew what she was thinking right now, she'd never hear the end of it. John Harrington would be perfectly happy if his daughter became a dried-up spinster. Ah, but she wasn't planning on that. She was ready to have a relationship and have *sex*. Frequently.

Fishing out her keys from her purse, she emerged into the cool, night air on the top deck of the parking structure. The parking lot was mostly deserted. The mall had closed about half an hour ago. She headed to her sporty black car, admiring the simple lines that hid a monster of an engine under the hood.

An agonized moan echoed in the empty lot.

Frowning, Paige stopped, uncertain if she'd heard correctly. Then it came again. There was a dark van parked a few feet in front of her. It sounded like it was coming from there. Approaching on silent feet, Page froze in shock at the sight that greeted her.

A woman sprawled on the cold pavement. Her blouse was torn and her lower body was naked. Remnants of a skirt lay on either side, her underwear cut to pieces. A man stood over her, a knife in his hand, the metal glinting dully as blood dripped on the floor. The woman's eyes found Paige.

"H-help me," she whispered.

The man slowly turned. Paige glimpsed cold gray eyes now trained on her.

"Oh, God."

At her horrified words, he headed for her.

Paige broke out of the trance she was in. Dropping the shopping bags she carried, she started to run. As fast as her feet could take her, she made for the stairwell on one end of the parking structure. Her heart hammered in her chest as she navigated the stairs, terror clogging her throat. She could hear his heavy footsteps getting closer, gaining on her. *No, please no. Don't let him catch me.*

She tripped on one of the steps and slammed against the concrete wall. Pain exploded in her shoulder and she lost her breath. With a terrified sob, she staggered to her feet, grabbed her fallen purse and took the steps as fast as she could. She heard laughter echoing behind her. *He was laughing at her.* Reaching the ground floor, she grasped the cold knob of the metal door and pushed it open, hearing it slam against the wall with a loud thud. Spotting the guard shack at the end of the drive, she ran and never looked back. Tears streamed down her face as she pounded on the window.

The security guard opened the door and looked at her with concern.

"Please," she gasped. "Help me."

He came out and pulled her up. "What's wrong, miss?"

"There's a man," she began, fear clogging her throat and her vision blurred by tears. She clenched her fists around his arms. "He...he..."

"Calm down, miss. Tell me what happened."

"He killed a woman on the third-floor level," she managed to get out. "I saw him and he's right behind me."

The security guard took out his radio and called for assistance, asking the dispatcher to call 911. He glanced behind her. "Don't be scared. You're safe now. There's nobody coming after you."

Paige dared to look, expecting to see the man in a long trench coat and cold gray eyes. There was nobody.

The drive was empty.

Chapter One

Paige pulled her cap lower over her face and huddled deeper in the plush leather seat of her father's luxury sedan. She stared out the window, the gray day matching her mood perfectly.

She rubbed her shoulder. The bruise was fading, but not the memory. Not for the first time, she wondered how fate could have brought her to that spot at the exact moment to witness somebody's life being taken.

"I will not tolerate any arguments, Paige," her father was saying as he negotiated the morning rush-hour traffic. His glance warned that his patience was at an end. "It's your insistence upon living in that neighborhood that brought this on. If you weren't so damn stubborn, you could be living in a nice, safe area instead of in the middle of a crime-ridden city."

Paige sighed. It was an old argument between the two of them. Her father was like a dog with a bone. He just won't let this one go. "Dad, my work takes up most of my time. Living two blocks away from the hospital is a matter of practicality, not stubbornness."

John Harrington snorted. "Don't even start with me, young lady. We are going to see my friend and get this matter taken care of."

His *friend* was the police commissioner, and the matter to be taken care of was her protection. As the only witness to a violent murder, her father insisted that she had to be protected until the suspect was found and arrested. Paige had already sat down with the detectives assigned to the case and had dutifully described the killer to the sketch artist. Thanks to her photographic memory, she was able to recall minute details that proved invaluable. But the suspect remained elusive.

"Why would he come after me?" she argued, trying to keep irritation out of her voice. "I gave the police a pretty detailed description of him. I'd be willing to bet he's already left the state to avoid capture. Or he's probably hiding out in Mexico."

Her father shook his head. "For somebody so smart, you fail to grasp the gravity of the situation." The car glided to a smooth stop in front of police headquarters. "Your life might very well be in danger. Are you willing to risk it?" Without waiting for her to answer, he opened his car door and got out. Biting back a retort, she followed him up the stone steps. Her father was unstoppable when he was on a mission, so she might as well get this over with.

In a top-floor office a few minutes later, Paige sat stoically as her father discussed the case with the police commissioner. With growing horror, she listened as the two men agreed that a detective would be assigned to watch her.

"You can't be serious," she protested.

The grim faces that stared back at her deflated whatever hope she had of talking her way out of this situation.

"This is just a precaution, Paige. We don't know who this man is or his motives for the crime," Commissioner O'Neil explained. "As a former District Attorney, your father understands the need to take precautionary measures."

She turned to her father and implored in a calm tone, "This really isn't necessary, Dad. I doubt the police department can spare the manpower just to watch over me."

Her father listened to her impassively before turning to the Commissioner. "Paul?"

O'Neil cleared his throat. "In this instance, we have the perfect candidate for the job, Paige. He's a highly decorated detective, experienced, and most important of all, I trust him to do his job well." He gave a confident nod. "His caseload is clear for the moment and he's available."

Paige sensed that no matter what arguments she put forth, she'd be shot down. But she'd be damned if she'd just give up the precious independence she'd just won. "Dad, I have a job. I don't want to be closeted in a room somewhere with a detective to baby-sit me. I've cooperated fully with the police. There's no need to further disrupt my life."

"I'm not closeting you anywhere, young lady," her father countered. "Your life doesn't have to come to a grinding halt. That's precisely why I want you guarded and protected, so you can get on with your life until this killer is found."

Paige inhaled a calming breath. "For how long?"

"For as long as necessary," her father replied, equally calm.

O'Neil stepped in. "Paige," he began in a diplomatic tone, "you're our sole witness. We need you to make our case in court." He gave her a reassuring look. "I've got a whole team of detectives working on this case. It should break wide open soon—maybe in a matter of days."

She threw her father a determined frown. "You win, Dad. But I refuse to hide in my apartment or anywhere else, for that matter. I refuse to stop living my life just because a killer may or may not be after me."

He didn't even hesitate. "Agreed."

Her shoulders slumped as she watched her father shake hands with his old friend. Flinging her messenger bag diagonally across her body, she jammed her cold hands in her jeans pockets. She bit the inside of her cheek in an attempt to silence herself. There was no arguing with her father. If he wanted her to have a bodyguard, then she damn well would have one. She was lucky to have gotten the concessions she had. What the hell was he supposed to do, this detective who was going to watch her twenty-four hours a day? Was he supposed to follow her around as she worked in the hospital? This whole thing was ridiculous. This was another one of her father's overreactions. The police better find the killer, and soon, before this whole thing drove her crazy.

* * * * *

"What do you mean, I have to watch her twenty-four-seven?" Nick Santorelli demanded. "Captain, this is ridiculous. I'm a detective, not a babysitter."

Captain Ridgeway fixed him with a steely glare. "You're lucky you're still a detective, Santorelli. That stunt you pulled last week almost got you fired."

Nick hunched in his chair, scowling in frustration. "I had the perp, Captain. You know I had to do what I did."

Ridgeway snorted. "Yeah, breaking and entering is part of your job description." He exhaled loudly. "If the commissioner didn't know your old man, your ass would have been out on the street a long time ago. Look, I see a lot of potential in you. But you can't bend the rules all the time just to get your man. You've got to follow policy." He glowered at Nick. "Instead of giving you desk duty or foot patrol, the commissioner is giving you another chance with this assignment."

Nick grimaced. Ridgeway had him there. He was already skating on thin ice with the brass. "I have other cases pending."

"Not anymore," Ridgeway said. "As of this morning, they've all been reassigned. This is your one and only case."

"For how long?"

"As long as it takes. I've got people working hard on this case, Santorelli. The commissioner gave this top priority."

A heavy sigh came from Nick. "Great. Now I'm a babysitter."

Ridgeway appeared to hold back his temper with great effort, and popped a tablet of Tums in his mouth. "The doctor you're going to be babysitting is the sole witness to the murder that happened at the Downtown Shopping Center parking structure."

Nick had heard of that incident, a cold-blooded killing in a deserted parking lot. So far, the police had managed to keep it out of the headlines and there'd only been a brief mention of the incident in the news the other day. "A doctor, huh?" Nick asked with a wince. "Jeez, she probably looks just like my grandmother."

"*Thank you*, Detective."

At the sound of the husky voice, Nick stood up and whirled around. Instead of the matronly figure he expected, a young woman stood behind him, looking none too pleased at what she'd undoubtedly heard. She had a cap pulled low over her face, so he couldn't really see what she looked like. She wore thin-rimmed glasses, her light brown hair pulled into a perky ponytail. A gray, oversized sweatshirt and loose jeans covered her body. All he could tell for sure was that she was about five foot six. Curves? He eyed her critically. Even through the shapeless sweatshirt, he could see the outline of her breasts.

Interesting.

His gaze went back to her face. Behind the glasses, she had large jade-green eyes. He couldn't discern any makeup on her face, but her skin had a soft, translucent sheen and looked silky smooth.

Very touchable.

Her ruby lips glistened damply, though they were free of any lipstick. The full curves looked sensuous and inviting. With a small frown, he tried to peer closer, his curiosity piqued. From where he stood, she was attractive. But the clothes, the cap, and the overall Plain Jane look hid the fact. Why would a woman deliberately choose to downplay her looks?

With a brief look of distaste at the cup she held in her hand, the young woman placed the thick, steaming cup of what appeared to be mud on top of the captain's desk.

"That stuff will kill you," Nick commented casually, a grin tugging at his lips.

Captain Ridgeway cleared his throat. "Dr. Paige Harrington, this is Nick Santorelli."

"Detective," she acknowledged coolly, before turning to Captain Ridgeway. "I thank you, Captain, for granting my father and the commissioner's request. "However, it's obvious that Detective Santorelli is not pleased at being saddled with me."

Nick opened his mouth to refute her statement, but the good doctor kept right on talking. Her aristocratic nose rose a notch. "I believe it would be to everyone's advantage if you would be so kind as to find somebody more suited to the task at hand."

Meow. The princess had claws. Nick fought to keep a grin off his face.

"That won't be necessary." He pinned Nick with a meaningful stare. "Dr. Harrington's father is a former District Attorney, who happens to be a close friend of the commissioner."

Nick bit back a sigh. "I apologize for my comments, Dr. Harrington. I didn't mean for you to hear what I said."

Her lips tightened. "I think everybody on the floor heard you, Detective."

Dull color suffused his cheeks. The woman had a sharp tongue.

"Well, Santorelli, I don't have to remind you that this case is your *only* case. As long as the perp is out there, Dr. Harrington's life is in danger. Any questions?" His tone implied there better not be any.

She was staring at him like he was the lowest worm in the entire world. Not a good sign. Nick felt like the biggest heel this side of the Pacific. At that moment, Commissioner O'Neil strode into the cramped office with a tall, distinguished-looking man. Ridgeway stood up and shot Nick a warning look that spoke volumes. Nick didn't move, just observed the new arrivals and caught the glance the silver-haired man threw Paige.

"So this is where you disappeared to. I told you to wait for us," he said in mild rebuke.

A brief shrug lifted her shoulders under her loose sweatshirt. "I needed some coffee."

"I trust everything is settled?" O'Neil asked the Captain.

Ridgeway nodded. "Yes, Sir. Nick Santorelli is more than capable of watching Dr. Harrington."

The commissioner turned to Nick. "I'm glad you understand the gravity of the situation, Detective. It is imperative that Dr. Harrington be protected until this man is caught."

He nodded respectfully. "I understand completely, Sir."

Harrington spoke to his daughter. "Would you excuse us for a moment, Paige?"

Her glance flicked from her father to Nick, then back again. With a curt nod, she walked out of the office and stood right next to window, looking at them through the glass. There was a mutinous tilt to her lips.

As soon as the door closed, Harrington faced Nick. "As you can see, my daughter is hardly pleased with this situation, Detective. But she *will* give you her full cooperation."

Commissioner O'Neil glanced at Captain Ridgeway. "You've cleared his schedule, Ridgeway? I want him full-time on this case."

"Yes, Sir. As of this moment, Santorelli's sole responsibility is to ensure Dr. Harrington's safety."

The commissioner nodded. "I'm confident you'll do a good job protecting Paige, Santorelli."

"I'll do my best, Sir."

"I don't have to tell you how important my daughter is to me. I'll do anything to protect her. I'm entrusting you with her life. Don't fail me."

Nick met his gaze directly. "You can rely on me, Mr. Harrington."

Harrington stared at him for long moments before nodding. "Very well. Anything you need, let me know." He turned to Ridgeway and extended his hand. "I would appreciate it if you would keep me apprised of any new developments, Captain."

Ridgeway clasped his hand. "No worries on that score, Mr. Harrington. You'll know as soon we get any leads on the case. Right now, my other detectives are running down all possible angles and checking out numerous tips."

Nick's gaze slid to Paige, who stared at them through the window. Something flickered in her eyes but it was gone quickly. He tuned out the conversation going on around him. He was a detective, for heaven's sake. Now he was supposed to be a bodyguard? His lips twisted. What the hell had he gotten himself into?

Paige bit her lip as she looked at the men gathered inside the small, stuffy office. Her father looked serious, talking in turn to the captain, the commissioner and of course, the detective. Nick Santorelli, the man who was supposed to guard her twenty-four hours a day for as long as necessary.

He was big. Standing next to her father, he stood straight and tall, about six-four. With his plain black shirt stretched taut against his muscled chest, and well-worn jeans lovingly hugging his butt, he oozed sex appeal. He wasn't perfectly sculpted or model gorgeous, but rather rugged and masculine. The sharp angles of his face and the high slash of his cheekbones were the perfect foil for his square jaw. And those lips. No man should have such sensual, full lips. Add thick dark hair to his Italian good looks and Paige was instantly hit by a forceful physical attraction.

Her bodyguard was a *stud.*

She bit back a sigh. *Here we go again.* So far, all the attractive men she'd encountered recently had been in one official capacity or another. Her lack of a social life sadly limited the kind of men she came across. The doctors at the hospital were old, married or going through a divorce. Her lips twisted. Slim pickings there. Even the younger nurses in the hospital had a more interesting and exciting life than she did. They constantly bragged about their boyfriends and sexual exploits.

But not her. Dr. Paige Harrington was too busy to even have a sex life. For years, she'd avoided men and the complication they represented out of necessity. School had been her priority. Nick Santorelli was exactly the kind of man she'd shied away from in the past. He was one of the too attractive, too masculine, too sexual men that an inexperienced girl like her could never hope to attract. He was the kind of man who made a woman want to be naughty and wicked, who would tie a woman up and make love to her until she begged for mercy.

But lately, she'd been feeling more and more that she wanted to *be* that kind of woman. She wanted to break out of the cocoon that had surrounded her all her life. She longed to indulge in a purely sexual affair—damn the consequences. Wasn't it about time she enjoyed herself? *Definitely.*

In fact, plans for the new Paige were already in motion. She'd gone on more dates lately than she ever had before. She was determined to expand her sexual experiences. Soon, the twenty-six year old doctor who'd had sex a grand total of two times would no longer exist. Her cheeks reddened. It was sort of embarrassing but she didn't care. She'd already made up her mind to sleep with Dan, the accountant her friend Georgina had introduced to her. They had gone out on two dates and hit it off well. Dan was kind and thoughtful, and a pleasant kisser. In her opinion, he was a good candidate to jumpstart her sex life. And the third date was the charm. She *expected* to sleep with Dan on their next date. It was all part of the grand plan to start *living* her life.

When she saw her father shake hands with Nick Santorelli, she knew the deal had been sealed. This hunk of a detective was now assigned to protect her. Her eyes followed the play of muscles on Nick's back as he extended his hand. He was built but not bulging, just lean and strong. The overall package was put together just right, from the casual shirt to the denim jeans. He looked…too good.

A sharp stab of arousal hit her low in the belly. Looking at him made her feel warm all over. Her nipples tightened beneath the lace of her bra. She shook her head. *I've deprived myself for too long.* That's why she was reacting this way to him, the first sexy man she'd come across in a long time. So what if he was bound to mess up her plans in a big way? So what if she was more attracted to him than she'd ever been to Dan? She could handle this situation. Her father had said this didn't have to interfere with her life. *He's damn right it won't.*

Lingering frustration made her turn away. Sometimes she hated being the only daughter of a powerful, influential man. She was the child they'd never expected, coming late in life. Paige understood his need to protect her. It was his insistence that she should be watched twenty four seven that grated on her nerves. She'd worked too hard for her independence for it to be taken away like this.

How was she going to stand being with the sexy detective all day? Her gaze strayed once again to the tight buttocks encased in jeans. How was she supposed to behave around him when she couldn't stop looking at his butt? This was not good, not good at all.

She looked at his hands. They were big. The fingers were long and thick. If what they said about a man's hands was true, then Nick Santorelli must be impressive all over. Her cheeks flamed. *Stop thinking about that.* What should a sexually frustrated doctor do in a situation like this? *Proceed with the plan.* Sleep with Dan in order to calm the raging, horny woman inside her.

*****

Paige struggled to keep her composure as she followed her father and the Commissioner to the front of the building. At seventy-five, her father still walked tall and proud, in remarkably good shape for his age. Her heart softened. If having a bodyguard gave him some peace of mind, then she would have to give in. His only thought was her safety.

The hairs on the back of her neck stood up. A huge shadow loomed over her shoulder.

"Where are we going, Doc?"

Paige stopped short, turning to the man whose deep voice slithered over her skin like a caress. Nick's voice was as smooth as perfectly aged whisky. "I have to go to work, Mr. Santorelli. As you're tasked with the boring assignment of watching over me, I suppose you're coming to work with me as well?" she asked, her voice laced with more than a hint of irritation.

In stark contrast, his tone was controlled and calm. "Look, I don't like this situation either, but sniping at me isn't going to make it easier. Since we're both in this together, what do you say we try to get along and work as a team?"

She colored fiercely. He made her feel like a petulant child. Straightening to her full height, she looked at him directly. "I apologize. This whole thing has upset me and I'm afraid I've taken it out on you."

He grunted. "Don't worry about it. Why don't you tell me where you work and I'll drive you?"

Paige frowned. "You don't have to drive me. I can catch a ride with my father."

The detective didn't bother to mask the sigh that blew from between his lips, and his tone was laced with impatience when he spoke. "It'd make my job easier, Doc, if you and I are in the same car. That way, you can bring me up to speed on your daily schedule and we can talk about the case."

Evidently, her father had overheard their conversation. John Harrington shook the Commissioner's hand goodbye and walked over to them. "Detective

Santorelli's right, Paige. I suggest you ride along with him and get acquainted." He gave her a kiss and murmured goodbye, admonishing her to call him later, before walking to his car.

Her lips tightened. With her father taking his side, she felt like a nitwit. "Fine." She followed the detective to a blue, nondescript sedan parked at the front of the building. He reached for the door handle the same time she did, and opened the door for her. Surprise, surprise. The detective was a gentleman.

"My mom was old-school," he murmured close to her ear. "She taught her sons to open doors for ladies."

"Thank you," she muttered, as she settled into the worn, leather seat. She stared straight ahead as he got in on the driver's side. Every time she breathed, she inhaled a subtle mixture of tangy aftershave and soap. The roomy car suddenly felt small and cramped. He filled it with his overwhelming masculine energy. What was wrong with her? In her line of work, she'd seen more classically handsome men than him. What made him so special? Unconsciously, she shifted closer to the door.

With a flick of his wrist, Nick turned the ignition and the engine purred smoothly. "So where to, Doc?"

"I work at County Hospital. It's on—"

"I know where it is." With a brief look over his shoulder, he slid smoothly into traffic.

Paige gripped the strap of her bag tightly. Even the way he held the steering wheel spoke of confidence. His fingers were long and thick, the nails cut short and blunt. Why, oh why, was she obsessing with this man's hands? Turning her red face toward her window, she stared resolutely at the passing scenery.

"How old are you?"

She grimaced. Here it was, the question she'd had to endure all her life. "I'm old enough to be a doctor."

Nick's eyebrows rose at her curt tone. "You look young," he observed. They stopped at a red light and he glanced at her expectantly.

Obviously he wasn't going to drop the subject. "I'm twenty-six."

"That's too young to have graduated from medical school and to be a—" he trailed off, a question in his eyes.

"Trauma surgeon," she supplied stiffly, staring straight ahead.

"Trauma surgeon, huh?" he echoed. "Very impressive. So if you're twenty-six, then you must have graduated early," he pressed on, clearly curious.

Paige muttered her answer, hoping that the green light would divert his attention. But she wasn't that lucky. She felt the quick glance he gave her.

"What was that?"

Her lips thinned in irritation. "I was sixteen when I graduated from college."

Another red light appeared, and they came to a smooth stop. Paige groaned inwardly. They must have hit all the red lights from the station to the hospital. She squirmed in her seat. They were in the middle of the morning rush-hour traffic, surrounded by vehicles of all sizes driven by angry, honking drivers. Inside the car, the atmosphere was quiet, hushed. It didn't matter that he irritated her with his probing question, she was still acutely aware of his big body sitting no more than a few inches away from her.

Out of the corner of her eye, she looked at him. His thick dark hair looked soft as it brushed the nape of his neck. Her gaze wandered down the length of his body. He looked entirely capable of protecting her.

"It must have been difficult not being around kids your age."

Interrupted from her thoughts, she reacted with surprise. "Usually people comment on my being 'freakishly smart' to have graduated so early."

He gave her a quick glance. "I think that's obvious. It must have been hard to cope with the pressure."

She shrugged, reminding herself not to notice how warm his chocolate brown eyes were. "I got used to it."

"Tell me about the murder."

Ugly memories came rushing back. "I told the other detectives everything I saw. I really don't want to talk about it again."

"There might be details that you remember now that you didn't then. It helps to talk about it," he prodded. "I need to know exactly what happened."

Projecting an outward calm that she really didn't feel, she recounted the violent events of that night. "It was around 9:30 at night. I was walking to my car in the parking structure when I heard a strange moaning sound."

"You moved toward the sound," he prompted.

"Yes, I did." She took a fortifying breath. "He was standing over her, a knife in his hand." A shudder skittered through her body. "She was still alive. I must have made a sound, because she turned to look at me and begged me to help her."

He pulled into the hospital parking lot and turned off the engine. "I know it's difficult, but I need to know the facts."

"I can't forget her eyes. They were open wide and—and I saw her life drain away. I will never forget that," she said quietly.

He placed a hand over hers, warm and reassuring. Small sparks of electricity raced over her skin at the contact. With a jerk, she pulled away from him. "He looked at me too, and he looked…evil. Then I ran. That's all I remember."

"What did he look like?"

"He was tall, wearing a long overcoat. Light hair. Gray eyes." She paused. "Cold gray eyes."

"If you see him again, you'll be able to recognize him?"

How could she forget the face of a killer? "Definitely."

"Are you okay?" he asked with a gentleness that surprised her.

"I'm all right." She checked the time on her watch and gripped the door handle. "I need to go in. I'm covering for a doctor who's attending a conference today. My shift starts in ten minutes."

He got out of the car and opened her door. "Let's go."

Paige blinked up at him. "Where are you going?"

He grinned, his eyes crinkling at the corners. "I go where you go, Doc."

"Mr. Santorelli—"

"Nick."

She got out of the car and craned her neck to look up at him. God, he was tall. "Nick. I'll be here for quite a while. I think I'm pretty safe inside the hospital, don't you?"

"Probably," he conceded. "But it's better if you get used to having me around, Doc. Until this guy is caught, I'm going to be your shadow."

Damn it. "Wouldn't you prefer to just come back for me later?"

"Don't worry. I'll stay out of your way. You won't even know I'm here."

Paige seriously doubted that. Like she could ignore him. Head held high, she marched to the entrance of the hospital. She couldn't help but notice a few nurses throwing Nick admiring looks. To her annoyance, he flashed them a smile. She tried to disguise her irritation, but was afraid she wasn't totally successful. Lengthening her stride, she headed for the doctor's lounge to change into her scrubs. When she came out, she was startled to find Nick standing right next to the door, leaning against the doorjamb. He just gave her a grin and followed her down the busy hallway to the emergency room.

Paige came to a dead stop and whirled around to face him. "I think it would be better for you to find somewhere to sit and not follow me around." She glanced at her watch and repeated her earlier suggestion with a hopeful expression. "Or you can come back for me when my shift is over." *So I can concentrate on work.*

"Nothing doing, Doc. But if it makes you happy, you can point me to an area where I can sit and still keep you in my sights."

The emergency room was already bustling with people waiting to be seen. Doctors and nurses scurried from gurney to gurney, treating patients in varying degrees of sickness. Tilting her head, she indicated a small waiting area. "That's the only place you can sit and wait for me. Please don't get in the way."

"Wouldn't dream of it, Doc," was his mocking reply.

Paige turned away and went directly to the triage area. County Hospital had taken on more and more patients since budget cuts instituted by the state had necessitated the closing of many free clinics. Most low-income patients that relied on the state to provide them with much needed health care automatically went to County.

Pushing Detective Santorelli to the back of her mind, Paige concentrated on work. In moments, she was occupied with treating a nine-month-old baby who'd suffered a "fall." One look at the tearful, frantic mother with a bruise darkening her left eye told Paige the whole story. Her lips tightened. This was most likely another case of domestic abuse, with the child caught in the middle.

Days like these, she wondered how she could ever harden herself to the ugly realities of life. But even as she thought it, she already knew the answer. She was a doctor and her job was to save lives and help people heal. Paige made a note on the chart to refer the mother to the county's domestic abuse crisis center. She examined the wailing infant, tamping down the anger and frustration she felt. She murmured soothingly to the baby, gratified when she stopped crying. She interviewed the mother at length while examining the baby, carefully gleaning the events that had brought them here, along with the baby's medical history. *Keep emotion out of it.* Gently testing the baby's responsiveness, she examined her thoroughly before ordering a lab workup. By the time she was done, the mother and child were a great deal calmer. Paige walked to the nurses' station and wrote her notes on the chart before briefly putting in a call to the police to report the likely abuse of the infant. This was a part of her job she hated, but it was necessary. Neglecting to report the abuse of a child could mean life and death in many cases. When she hung up, she felt better knowing the police were on their way to talk to the mother.

Even without looking, Paige knew Nick was sitting on the hard, uncomfortable chairs of the waiting room. She could actually feel his gaze on her. Resisting the temptation to turn around and look at him, she focused on writing orders on the chart. Now wasn't the time to think of the sinfully sexy detective assigned to be her bodyguard.

Chapter Two

Nick shifted in the cheap, plastic chairs in the hospital emergency room. He didn't bother to hide the fact that he was staring at Paige. Her hair was pulled back in a ponytail and she was wearing eyeglasses. The green scrubs she wore were regulation, functional and sexless. Yet his body stirred. Dr. Paige Harrington was a babe.

What the hell was wrong with him? Why did he suddenly have the hots for a doctor who deliberately underplayed her looks? His tastes had always run to sexy as all get-out women. Now he was sitting in the middle of a crowded emergency room, sporting a huge erection for a woman in shapeless clothing. He must be losing his mind. Yes, that must be it. This assignment was driving him insane. The Doc was driving him batty.

Nick grimaced and surreptitiously adjusted himself. Sitting in the car with her had been torture. She smelled damn good. Talking to her had been just as hard. Her voice was husky, sexy. Damn it, how could he be so turned on by such a little slip of a woman who was way too smart for him? Her IQ was probably in the genius range and he was willing to bet that she was a card-carrying member of Mensa.

That thought didn't deter his traitorous body. Time and time again, his gaze had been drawn to her tempting red lips. When her tongue flicked out to lick the full curves, he'd almost groaned out loud. What the hell was the matter with him? He'd had a hell of a time talking to her while imagining her lips doing something else entirely. Like sucking his dick. There was no way in hell she couldn't have noticed what she was doing to him. But apparently she hadn't, for she'd sat there in the car, stiff as a board and completely unaware of his discomfort.

Again and again he'd found himself looking at her chest, trying to discern what was underneath the loose sweatshirt. Hell, he was a man, and she aroused his curiosity. *Among other things.*

Paige Harrington was a mystery he wanted to unravel.

She'd fiddled with the strap of her bag as she sat in the car, and her hands drew his gaze. They were slim and graceful, the nails cut short, unadorned by nail polish. He could easily imagine her hands wrapped around his cock, slowly stroking him up and down as her lips learned his length and memorized his shape.

Nick stifled a groan. This was getting damned uncomfortable. His cock was pushing insistently against the crotch of his jeans. Its stiff length was visible through the rough material. Anybody looking at him would know right away he was thinking inappropriate thoughts.

He looked up. Across the aisle from him, a young woman in a skimpy top and short skirt was staring at him. Her heavily lined eyes dropped with obvious interest to the front of his jeans before coming back up to meet his. Her eyebrows rose in silent invitation. Her pink, pierced tongue traced her lips in a suggestive manner.

Her breasts, full and spilling over her top, didn't even stir him. *Okay, that's weird.*

Her legs, bare and exposed, didn't fire up his imagination. *Something's definitely wrong with me.*

Nick pushed himself off the chair and strode to the nearest window, looking out at the smoggy day that once again surrounded Los Angeles. The downtown streets were crowded and congested. It was the price you paid for living in a large, sprawling city like this one.

"Hellooo."

At that murmured greeting, he turned and found the young woman standing way too close for comfort. He schooled his face into a quiet, polite expression.

If it was possible, she brushed even closer to him. "I thought I'd keep you company. You looked pretty lonely back there." She drew a fingertip down the front of his shirt. "Waiting in the emergency room is the pits. Maybe you and I could entertain each other?"

There was no doubt at all what she meant by "entertain". Nick couldn't believe she was trying to solicit him inside a hospital, of all places. But a working girl was always on the prowl, he guessed. It would serve her right if he slapped handcuffs on her and called vice to pick her up. With a rueful grin, he took her wandering hand in his. He had opened his mouth to let her down easy when he was interrupted by a loud clearing of a throat.

Paige was standing a few feet away, looking none too pleased, her arms crossed. Her glance flicked from him to the young woman, finally ending on their clasped hands. Those delicious lips tightened with displeasure. "Excuse me for interrupting." Her tone was like a gust of icy wind. "I came over to suggest that you might want to get a cup of coffee or something to eat, but I see you're already occupied."

The young woman in his arms had the nerve to throw her head back and laugh. "She doesn't seem too happy. Are you hers?"

A grin tugged at Nick's lips at her audacity. For some reason, he felt driven to further annoy Paige. Payback maybe, for giving him a hard-on that wouldn't go away? His look was utterly sexy as he glanced at a seething Paige then back to the young woman who was practically in his arms.

"Thanks for the suggestion, Doc. I'll keep it in mind."

It was fun to watch Paige's eyes widen in disbelief at his dismissal. She stomped away, anger visible in every stiff muscle in her body. He chuckled as he gently pushed the young woman away and pulled out his badge. "I'm going to try to forget that you're soliciting in a hospital, sweetheart."

An artful pout pulled blood-red lips together. "Soliciting? I never said anything about payment." Her smile was laced with invitation. "Maybe we can have some fun in a quiet closet somewhere? It'll be on the house." At the small shake of his head, she shrugged philosophically. "Sure you won't change your mind?"

"Positive." His tone was firm. "Now unless you have real business here in the hospital, I'd suggest you leave."

"My friend broke her arm," she answered sweetly. "So yes, I have real business here in the hospital." She walked away, her hips swaying under her short skirt. But not before she gave him one last regretful look over her shoulder.

Nick searched for Paige in the crowded room. He found her in a corner, writing on a chart, frowning with concentration. Suppressing a smile, he headed her way. "Doc."

She didn't even look up. "Go away, Detective. I'm busy."

"Paige—"

Her head whipped up, her eyes flashing deep green in irritation. "Am I mistaken or are you assigned to protect me? I thought you were on duty, Detective."

Boy, he liked it when she was spitting mad. He felt his cock stirring once again. "It was a little harmless thing, no big deal."

"Whatever," she said in dismissal, training her eyes on the chart she held.

He moved closer. "Would you like to join me for a cup of coffee?" His tone was low, intimate.

She stiffened. "I'm not due for a break until later."

He caught a whiff of her enticing scent and lessened the distance separating them even more. "I'll wait for you then."

Paige took a wary step back. "Don't wait for me. Like I said, you're free to go and come back for me later."

"I didn't encourage her." He didn't know why, but he felt compelled to explain.

Her eyebrow arched. "I really don't care about that. However, I would appreciate it if you would keep your mind on the job." Her tone was polite and freezing. "If this will be difficult for you, maybe we should call the Captain and make other arrangements."

Christ, she was so fucking prickly. He loved it. "Can't get rid of me that easy, Doc."

She lifted her chin. "I certainly hope it won't be too difficult for you to keep your womanizing at bay."

"Womanizing?" Nick threw his head back and laughed. The hot color that flooded her cheeks was delightful. "I'll try to rein in my baser urges, Doc. Besides, I've never gone for hookers." He watched as realization set in. Shaking his head in amusement, he left her staring at him as he made his way back to the chairs and assumed his watchful position.

This attraction he was feeling for her was making him uneasy. It required no effort on her part to get his cock to stand at attention, while the blatant invitation from the sexy hooker produced no reaction at all. What the hell was the matter? He looked down at his offending organ in disgust. A few words from Paige and his cock was up and begging. *Dangerous.* He even found her prickly attitude a major turn-on.

She was a puzzle he wanted to figure out.

Other women he knew flaunted and emphasized their assets. But not Paige. He didn't understand why. Was it to avoid attention? *Hmm. Maybe.*

His hands itched to touch her, to smooth back the wisps of hair that escaped her ponytail. He wanted to take off her glasses and look into her deep green eyes. He wanted to whip off her loose clothing and expose her true shape. Maybe then he'd stop wondering and thinking about her. Maybe then his cock wouldn't be so hard every time she was near.

* * * * *

Paige turned away in mortification, dragging her eyes away from the detective's tight behind. What was wrong with her? She had behaved like a jealous girlfriend! It wasn't any of her business if he flirted with another woman. Why did the sight of Nick Santorelli talking to the skimpily dressed young woman spark a sudden unexplainable anger in her? Before she could stop herself, she had marched straight over to him and almost berated him in front of a dozen people sitting in the waiting room. *Oh God, what must he think of her?* She'd behaved like a shrew. A *jealous* shrew.

"How stupid can I be?" she muttered softly. "I couldn't have announced it in any plainer terms that I find him attractive." She picked up the chart once more, but the words just swam in front of her. "Get a grip. Get yourself under control."

Nick Santorelli was assigned to protect her. He was going to be around her a lot. It would behoove her to find some way to control her feelings. It wouldn't do to show him that she was attracted to him. Getting involved with Nick would be too complicated. What she needed to do was forget the silly attraction she had for him and stick to the plan. Stick to Dan.

It was easier said than done. She imagined his big hands cupping her breasts, teasing her nipples into hard crests, his muscular legs curving around hers as he held her tightly in his arms. How would his cock feel and taste? She flushed.

How many times had she overheard the nurses talking about having sex with their boyfriends? Of positions and acts that she'd never even dreamed of? She'd been embarrassed, but had eavesdropped with fascination.

She'd love to do those things with Nick.

Vivid images of the two of them flooded her mind—bodies tangled in sex-mussed sheets, his cock going in and out of her pussy, her pleasure-roughened voice screaming his name…

"Dr. Harrington?"

Paige jumped. The image vanished. "I'm sorry?"

The nurse looked at her with concern. "Are you all right, Doctor? Do you need anything?"

A cold shower. "I'm fine, thank you," she said out loud.

Detective Santorelli was a distraction she didn't need. A furtive glance confirmed Nick sitting in the chair, no sign of the young woman anywhere. Relief rushed through her, a feeling she refused to analyze at the moment. Squaring her shoulders, she headed toward the little girl crying in a curtained exam room. She needed to get back to work and forget about the detective whose gaze was like a physical touch.

*****

The hospital cafeteria was bustling when Paige sat down to lunch with Georgina Hayes. Georgina was an anesthesiologist and one of the first friends she'd made when she came to work at County. In her early thirties, voluptuous and attractive, Georgina was her complete opposite. Maybe that was why they got along together so well.

"So who's the stud following you around?" Georgina asked, chewing on her club sandwich.

Paige tried not to let her gaze slide to Nick. He was standing patiently in line, waiting to pay for his food. "He's a detective assigned to watch me."

A delighted grin spread across her friend's face. "Well, well. This is interesting." Georgina glanced over at Nick. "He looks delicious."

A light flush covered her cheeks. "If you say so."

"Come on, Paige," she chided. "Are you seriously going to sit there and tell me you don't find him attractive?"

Her answer was a noncommittal shrug. "He's okay, I suppose." *Liar*.

Georgina leaned forward. "You know, he'd be the perfect candidate to get you laid."

Paige choked on her sandwich. "Georgina!"

Blue eyes blinked innocently at her. "What? Is anything wrong with that? I thought we agreed that it was high time you got laid again. How long has it been?"

Her eyes darted around. "Too long," she muttered.

"See? I don't see anything wrong with considering him, Paige," Georgina stated.

She shook her head. "No. Not him."

"If you ask me—" her friend said in low, confiding tones, "—he'd be the one. He's with you twenty-four-seven. He's tall, dark and gorgeous." She leaned back and nodded wisely. "I'd pick him, if I were you."

"But you're not me," Paige countered. "I just don't think I have the courage to do it."

Georgina grinned. "To do *him*, you mean."

Paige shrugged and sipped her soda.

The curly reddish locks of Georgina's hair bounced on her shoulders as she swung her head around to look at Nick. "God, I'd do him in a minute."

Paige laughed. "You're shameless."

A perfectly shaped eyebrow rose. "There's nothing wrong with enjoying sex, Paige. God knows, I've had sex often enough. My ex, for all his faults, was great in bed. We did everything. And I mean *everything*."

"So why'd you divorce him?" Paige asked curiously.

Georgina snorted. "I drew the line when he wanted a threesome with his friend."

She shot her a disbelieving look. "You turned down a threesome?"

"I did that time. His friend was an asshole," she replied with an incorrigible grin. "Paige, sex is wonderful. Sex is fun. You need sex. Just because your first boyfriend didn't know what the hell he was doing doesn't mean you should shun sex forever."

"I know that, Georgie."

"You've buried your nose between medical books for too long. Life is passing you by," she declared.

"I'm only twenty-six," Paige said dryly. "Life hasn't exactly passed me by."

Georgina rolled her eyes. "I could tell you stuff that I did when I was your age that would shock you. But it's not too late for you. We can work on getting you some sex." She slid a regretful glance at Nick, who was now sitting a few tables away. "If you really don't want him to do you, then we'll have to stick to our original plan with Dan. When are you going out with him?"

"Tomorrow night. He's taking me to his favorite Peruvian restaurant. "

"Good," Georgina said with satisfaction. "Third date is the charm, Paige."

Now why did that bring a feeling of dread instead of anticipation? *It's just nerves.* It was natural to be nervous. She hadn't had sex in years.

Taking a sip of her soda, Georgie looked at her thoughtfully. "Don't worry. It'll be all right. Have you thought about what you're going to wear tomorrow night?"

She held up a hand. "I already have a dress."

Georgina rolled her eyes. "Is it long? Does it cover you from the neck down? Is it something that would be more suited for a nun?"

This was an old discussion between the two of them. "No."

"You have all the right equipment, Paige," Georgina argued. "You just need to enhance it."

"You know why I haven't."

With a huff, Georgina sat back. "I think it's ridiculous. Why do you have to hide behind eyeglasses and pretend to be a plain Jane? You're a great doctor, Paige. God knows, you're smarter than all the doctors here combined. You don't have to prove yourself anymore. They know what you can do. And believe me, they take you seriously."

Paige sighed. "Nevertheless, I'd prefer not to draw too much attention to myself."

"I think you've just gotten so used to hiding from everybody that you've convinced yourself it's the right thing to do." Georgina wiggled her eyebrows. "Don't you want to look and feel sexy?"

She shrugged. "Maybe. But definitely not here at work."

Her friend grinned with satisfaction. "Fair enough. Now for your date with Dan, will you please do me a favor and wear the dress that I brought for you? It's the perfect little black number. My mother gave it to me as a gift but it's a couple of sizes too small. What do you think?"

Paige nodded reluctantly.

"Go out with Dan and see what happens tomorrow night. Just go with the flow. And remember, enthusiasm always makes up for inexperience."

Once again, Paige's gaze was drawn to Nick. Though he was sitting two tables away, he attracted attention. He was one of those men who had an air of confidence about him. Her eyes caressed his thick, muscular thighs. She just knew that he would be good in bed. Dan the accountant was nothing like him. He was affable, gentle and easygoing. Tomorrow night she was probably going to end up in bed with Dan.

So why did that sound boring as hell?

Maybe Georgina was right. Maybe she should set her sights on Nick. God knows, she got all hot and bothered every time he happened to be near her. But would he want to have sex with her? Would he want to be the one to teach a twenty-six-year-old bookworm doctor the joys of sex?

He looked up and caught her looking at him. A slow, sexy grin pulled his lips apart. Paige hurriedly averted her eyes, cheeks flushed lightly. No. She'd better stick to Dan.

Georgie followed her gaze. "He won't be with you on your date, will he?"

With growing dismay, reality dawned on Paige. She groaned. "I can't go out on a date with him watching me the whole time. Damn it." She bit her lip worriedly. "Maybe I should just cancel with Dan?"

"You could," Georgina agreed, then went on. "But how hard would it be to convince the detective to let you loose for a few hours?"

"I don't know." Paige slid another surreptitious glance at Nick. "I could try, I suppose. All I know is I refuse to hide in my apartment for the duration. I mean, how do I even know if this…this killer is looking for me? They kept my name out of the papers. I haven't received any threats," she reasoned.

Her friend stared at her. "So what are you going to do?"

"I'm going to go out with Dan tomorrow night," Paige declared with determination. "Somehow I'll convince Detective Santorelli to leave me alone for a few hours." She needed to do this. Ever since she'd decided to change her life, she'd done everything according to her plan. And she wasn't about to mess with the plan just because a man out there may or may not be after her. If anything, witnessing the violent murder had taught her that life was too short not to enjoy. She was just going to have to figure something out tomorrow. There was no way she was going to miss out on her date with Dan. It would also be the perfect chance to get rid of this ridiculous infatuation she had with Nick.

Tomorrow, Paige Harrington was finally going to get lucky.

* * * * *

After a grueling day at work, all Paige wanted to do was go home, take a long, hot bath and sleep. As she sat in the car, all she could think of was the man sitting next to her. Soft music was playing on the radio, and the atmosphere was too close, too intimate for her to be comfortable. She looked out the window. Clouds covered the moon and fog had rolled in, wrapping the city in an eerie blanket of darkness.

It had been a long day, but he'd stayed. She didn't miss the relief that flashed quickly across his face when she finished for the night. "I told you not to wait for me," she reminded him in the silence of the car.

"Not complaining, Doc," he answered in a mild voice. "In fact, today reminded me of stakeouts. Now *that* always drove me crazy, never could stand sitting in the car for too long."

When he turned onto her street, he surveyed it critically. "Your father was right, you know. This is not the best place to live."

"It's close to where I work," she reasoned. Her loft was located inside one of the converted warehouses that lined the street. "It may not look like much, but its home. Most of the buildings here are newly converted apartments and townhomes. And the police have started more patrols around here." She glanced at him. "But I guess you know that."

Nick pulled up outside her building, glancing around before spotting an empty space and quickly slipping into it. "Lucky I found an empty spot," he muttered. "How's security?"

She shrugged. "It's adequate. You have to be buzzed in at the door and all outside doors are locked."

Nick glanced up and down the street while he rounded the car and opened her door. "Too dark," he criticized.

Paige slid her security card into the slot and waited for the buzzer to sound before she pushed the door open. She went to the bank of mailboxes and checked hers, pulling out a small pile of mail before heading to the elevator. She was aware of Nick checking out the hallway, trailing after her. He moved silently for a man his size.

Though she hated to admit it, she was glad he was around. He made her feel safe and secure. Coming home late at night was her least favorite thing to do. Contrary to what her father said, she'd always been conscious of her safety. What he didn't know was, more often than not, she was lucky enough to go home at the same time as two other people who worked at the hospital.

Ever since she'd witnessed the murder, she'd been aware of how easy it would have been for an intruder to target her. Maybe she could squeeze in some self-defense lessons in the meantime.

"Where do residents park?" he asked as they waited for the old elevator to make its way down.

"There's an underground parking structure," she replied absently. She stole a glance at his thick, wavy hair. The kind that would welcome a woman's fingers threading through the dark strands.

"I can already see security problems here."

'What do you mean?" she asked, paying little attention to what he was saying. His nose had a little bump, as if it had been broken a time or two. But instead of detracting from his overall look, it actually made him more appealing. He was gorgeous in a rough-hewn, realistic way. What he exuded was sex, plain and simple.

Should she go for great sex right away? Or go with a safer, more predictable choice like Dan? Maybe nice and easy was a better way to initiate a sex-starved twenty-six-year-old doctor into having a normal sex life. Yup. Maybe later when she was more experienced and surer of herself, she could go for somebody like Nick.

Feeling somewhat reassured by her mental decision, Paige rubbed the back of her head. She rolled her shoulders, the muscles protesting the exhaustion beating at her. A long, relaxing massage would do wonders for her.

"Coming home late at night like this, and pulling into an underground parking lot, is a disaster waiting to happen. Somebody could very easily run inside before the gate closes and surprise you."

She pulled up short and stared at him.

Nick returned her gaze steadily. "At this time of night, I'm sure it's virtually deserted. Even if you scream, I doubt anybody would hear you."

"I never thought of that." She tightened her grip on her messenger bag.

Nick noted her nervous gesture. "What are you going to do? Whack him on the head with that bag? You need to get mace and attach it to your keys. Any deterrent is better than nothing."

"I understand," she mumbled.

"You're lucky nothing has happened before now. First thing you have to do is look around, make sure nothing looks out of the ordinary. Be alert. Have your keys ready when you get out of the car." He paused. "Most important, don't get distracted."

"All right," she said with a nod. Nick's advice made sense and she knew it was only smart to listen to him. Paige followed him into the elevator and shrank back against the rear. He didn't say anything, just stood across from her. She fixed her gaze on the floor. It was moments like this when she wished she was sophisticated and witty. Instead, she had no idea what to say. She felt gauche. Not for the first time, she wished she'd learned the art of flirting that seemed to come naturally to other women. *I can recite complicated mathematical formulas in my head, but I get tongue-tied in the presence of a living, breathing stud.* How come she never felt like this with Dan? *Because Dan's nothing like Nick.* She stepped quickly from the elevator when it stopped on her floor and hurried down the well-lit hallway to her door.

He held out a hand. "Give me the key."

Paige frowned at the large hand he extended to her. "Is this really necessary? I'm sure nobody broke into my apartment. I mean, we're four floors up from ground level."

Nick waited, his hand extended, palm up.

With a long-suffering sigh, she dropped her keys on his palm and waited for his all clear sign before going inside. Her apartment was the place she loved the most. It was the mark of her independence. It was all the more important since she'd fought a lengthy battle with her father about living on her own. Now it was her home.

With a grateful smile, she turned to Nick. "I know this can't be easy for you, Detective," she began.

He raised an eyebrow. "Nick," he drawled.

"Nick," Paige repeated dutifully. "I'm sure, like me, you're hoping that they'll get the killer soon so we can go on with our normal lives. I appreciate everything you're doing for me. I guess I'll see you tomorrow?"

He grinned. "I'm sleeping right here."

She blinked at him through her glasses. "What?"

He crossed his arms in front of his chest. "I'm staying the night."

Paige was dumbfounded. He said it as if he did this every night. "B-but why?" she sputtered. "I'm home, I'm safe. I'll lock all the doors and windows. There's no need for you to do that." She paused, feeling the sticky fingers of panic clutching at her. "Besides, I only have one bedroom."

Nick eyed her couch. "That'll do."

She shook her head. "Really, this isn't necessary..."

He straightened to his full, intimidating height. "Listen, I was assigned to watch you twenty-four-seven. That means I stay with you all day, all night. Now, we can stand here arguing about it, or you can give me what I need to make a bed on the couch so you can hit the sack. You've had a long day."

Paige took in his implacable stance and knew it was useless arguing. Her lips tightening in annoyance, she stalked over to her linen closet and pulled out a thick blanket and a pillow. "What about clothes?" she asked.

His chocolate colored eyes gleamed with amusement. "Are you afraid you'll see me sleeping in the buff?"

She flushed. "Don't you need them?"

"I don't think anything of yours would fit me," he countered teasingly. Her narrowed eyes drew a chuckle from him. "I'll go down to my car. I have a duffel bag with a change of clothes in the trunk."

"Just in case the need arises?" she asked sweetly.

Nick grinned. "Actually, it's for when I go to the gym. Although it never hurts to be prepared, right? One never knows when one will get lucky." He pocketed her key and headed to the door. "I'll be right back."

Paige flushed. What had possessed her to say that? How on earth would she sleep tonight, knowing he was right outside her bedroom? She eyed the dainty couch. He wouldn't be comfortable on that. He was too big and too tall to fit. *Oh well,* she thought, without any trace of sympathy. It would serve him right if he was cramped and unable to sleep. Why wouldn't he listen to her and go home for the night? She was perfectly safe in her apartment. What could happen to her here?

She tossed the blanket and pillow on the couch and headed to her bedroom to take a shower. Then she remembered. There was only one bathroom in the apartment. Nick was going to have to go inside her room if he wanted to take a shower.

Paige groaned. Could things get any worse? *Oh, to hell with it.* She closed the door before quickly stripping off her clothes. He could wait until she was done with her bath. No way was she going to miss her nightly relaxing ritual just because her life had just been turned upside down.

She turned on the taps in the large tub and lit the candles littered around the edges. Next, she turned on her CD player and put on her favorite soothing jazz music. The soft strains rose and echoed around the room. The water swirled and bubbled as she poured in a small measure of her favorite scented bath oil. Soon, the soothing fragrance permeated the small bathroom.

Twisting her hair into a knot, Paige slid into the tub and released a blissful sigh. Shadows from the flickering candles danced along the wall. This was her favorite time of day. Her stiff muscles began to loosen up. If she didn't have this to look forward to at the end of her shift, she'd probably go crazy.

The tension slowly began to seep out of her. Now that she thought about it, it was better that he was staying the night. She couldn't deny that Nick made her feel safe. On the other hand, he was dangerous to her peace of mind. She was much too attracted to him.

Her lips twisted. It'd been her experience that men like Nick went for women who were sophisticated and well-versed in the games that men and women played. What did she know about that? Hardly anything at all. She'd been a smart kid who'd been accelerated into higher grades at an early age. She'd never had the chance to interact with boys her age.

In high school, she'd been the youngest in her class. She grimaced at the memory. She'd still had on braces in her yearbook picture, for God's sake. School dances were an exercise in torture, because she could only watch from the sidelines. She finally just stopped going and stayed home to hit the books.

College wasn't any better. She was known as the genius kid, the one who went through her four-year college in two years before going on to medical school. She was *nerd* personified. Boys? Not in the picture at all.

How many times had she wished she could just be normal? She missed out on a lot of things. She'd had sex with one man, and that wasn't anything worth remembering. For months Georgina had been pushing her to broaden her sexual horizons. Her friend had done her utmost to show her what she'd missed, and was still missing by living a reclusive life. So Paige made the decision to make some major changes, namely to actually *have* a life and find a man to date and have sex with. She'd picked Dan. Now Nick was in the picture. He made her feel weird and funny inside, but he was way out of her league.

With a deflated sigh, she closed her eyes. Maybe she was attracted to him because he was different from all the other men she'd known, professionally or socially. Besides, it was entirely possible that their enforced togetherness would continue to feed this attraction she felt for him. So what could she do? *I need to focus on Dan. A man more suited for somebody like me.*

*****

As soon as Nick heard her footsteps padding inside her room, he knocked on her bedroom door. "Paige?"

The door opened. There she stood, her hair clipped on top of her head, dressed in pink pajamas. With her face scrubbed clean and tinged a light rose, she looked much younger and adorable.

"You need to use the shower?" she asked in a polite tone.

She smelled heavenly. What the hell did she use? "You don't mind? It's been a long day and I'd like to clean up."

Paige stepped back and opened the door wider. "Of course. I'll be in the kitchen. Take your time." She went around him and headed to the kitchen, her feet encased in thick socks.

Nick stepped inside and looked around. Her queen-sized bed was immaculate and neat but not frilly or too feminine. A smile tugged at his lips. Evidently she liked pillows. There were a number of them on top of the thick down comforter. With reluctance, he tore his eyes from the bed and stepped into the bathroom.

To his surprise, it was large. A tiled bathroom counter and sink took up the length of one wall. On top of it was a wide array of lotions, shower gels and bath oils. Hmm. Which one made her smell so good?

Opposite that was a large sunken tub surrounded by candles of different sizes. There was a CD player next to the tub, no doubt the source of the sexy jazz music he'd heard earlier. He grinned. Well, what do you know? Paige Harrington liked to indulge in scented baths and sexy music. *Very interesting.*

He stepped into the shower and picked up her shampoo, wincing at the floral scent. He made a mental note to buy his own to use for next time. The sting of the hot water spray on his back was relaxing. He didn't know how long he stood there, just letting the water sluice over him. He stirred himself to turn the water off and towel himself dry. He normally slept naked but he decided he could sleep in his shorts. He grinned. He wouldn't want to offend the Doc.

He walked into the kitchen and found her looking through her mail. She looked up as he stopped in front of her. She kept her gaze on his face, studiously avoiding looking his bare chest. "All done?"

He gave her a slow grin. "All nice and clean. You want to check, Doc?"

"No, thank you," she answered in a prim voice. She looked back before she entered her bedroom. "Tell me, Detective. Under what circumstances could you be persuaded to leave me for a few hours?"

His answer was short and to the point, delivered in a tone that brooked no argument. "None."

A flicker of something quickly crossed her face before she politely murmured goodnight. For a moment, he wondered what she was up to. She wouldn't be so foolish as to try to get away from him, would she? *Nah.* She wasn't the type to pull a stunt like that.

With that thought, he settled on the small couch. He tossed and turned, trying to find a comfortable position. *Damn it.* Ridgeway owed him big time for this. He punched the pillow before lying back down. He thought of the big, roomy bed in her bedroom. What he wouldn't give to lie down on a plush, queen-sized bed right now. He turned once more, unable to stay in one position for long. After a few minutes, he gave up and lay on his back, closed his eyes and forced himself to go to sleep.

Chapter Three

Paige fidgeted in her chair while she worked up the courage to do what she needed to do.

She needed to ditch Nick so she could go out with Dan tonight.

All night long, she'd lain awake, unable to sleep. It was difficult trying to figure out a way to go alone. The implacable set of his face when she'd asked him last night told her she couldn't talk her way out of this one. He wasn't about to let her go anywhere without him.

She had to be sneaky and underhanded if she wanted to be able to go out with Dan tonight.

Her chair scraped the floor as she stood up. Outside, it was another smoggy, overcast Los Angeles afternoon. The weather matched her mood perfectly. She knew she was courting trouble with what she was about to do. The timing was lousy and the circumstances awful. However, her father *did* say her life didn't have to come to a standstill, didn't he? What else was she supposed to do? Nick was not going to leave her alone. Neither was he going to understand why she was so hell-bent on going on this date. He hadn't lived a reclusive, lonely life like she had. Georgie was right. If she wasn't careful, life would pass her by. Before she knew it, she'd be old and alone. With a grimace, she pushed her hair behind her ear. She could do this. She had to.

"Are you all right?"

Startled, she whirled around. She'd forgotten Nick was sitting on the couch. "I'm fine. Just thinking."

He gave her a curious look over the newspaper he'd been reading. "Are you sure? You seem to be a little jumpy today."

Paige forced a smile to her lips. "Sorry. It's work-related."

Nick looked at her thoughtfully. "You mentioned you had some errands to run?"

She nodded. "Let me just grab my purse. I'll be ready in a couple of minutes." Her heart thudded. She was so nervous. She'd never been a good liar. Any moment now, he was going to figure out she was up to something and blow her plans to pieces. Avoiding his gaze, she went to her bedroom and grabbed her purse and the shopping bag on the floor. *I can do this. I can do this.* Over and over again, she repeated the mantra in her head.

She'd also told herself repeatedly since she got up this morning, *ignore Nick*. Ignore how the cotton of his shirt stretched taut across those impressive shoulders. Ignore how he could make a simple pair of jeans look so good. Ignore his long, tanned fingers as he held his cup of coffee. Stop looking at his ass.

Think of Dan. Think of the man who could potentially be making love to you tonight. But instead of Dan's blond looks and easy smile, it was Nick's dark hair and striking face that came to her mind. *No. Not him.* Concentrate. Remember that you're doing all this so you can see Dan tonight. Not Nick, Dan. She was about to end three years of abstinence. To do that, she had to get away from her bodyguard.

Mentally squaring her shoulders, she grabbed her key from where it hung on the wall. Pasting a smile on her face, she turned to him. "Would you mind if I drove? I only get to do that on weekends."

He shrugged. "No problem."

"Thank you," she mumbled as she preceded him out the door. They were silent as they rode down the elevator to the parking garage. She waved to a couple of other tenants in the building as she walked to her car.

Nick lifted an eyebrow as he saw which one was hers. "I never would have thought you'd drive a car like this, Doc."

Paige deactivated the alarm to her black Porsche. "Why not?"

"Just didn't think you were the type. There's a lot of power under the hood."

"I've decided to make some changes in my life, Detective," she stated casually, if a little carefully. "This is one of them." She ran a caressing finger on the shiny paint. "It's about time I have some fun."

"Some fun," he muttered, folding his long length inside the car.

Paige grinned. He looked like he was trying to work out a puzzle. She stowed the shopping bag in the trunk before getting in the car.

Nick looked around the interior of the car. "Nice."

As always, the heady excitement of driving the powerful car began to weave its magic on her. "Yes, isn't it?" She flicked on the ignition and listened to the powerful purr of the engine. That was a sound she loved to hear. It was an indicator of the power that was at her fingertips. Exhilaration began to unfurl inside her. "Ready?"

He fastened his seat belt and nodded. Paige drove up the ramp to the gate and pulled out into early afternoon traffic. As usual, LA was in a gridlock. Their progress was a slow stop and go.

"Someday I'm going to take this car out in the open road," she mused out loud. "Just fly down the road."

Nick shook his head. "The highway patrol might have something to say about that."

Her fingers clenched on the smooth leather of the steering wheel. "The only time I feel free is when I'm behind the wheel." She glanced at him. "Have you ever felt that way?"

"You don't feel free, Paige?" he asked.

For a brief moment, the loneliness of her existence surfaced in her eyes. "Not really. Only lately have I been truly independent. I think it's about time I have some fun in my life." She turned the car onto the freeway. Stepping on the gas, she merged smoothly with the flow of traffic. Smiling at the surge of power from the purring engine, Paige expertly maneuvered around the other cars and gained speed. "I love driving this car." She whizzed by an old lady in an aging sedan.

"Jesus," Nick muttered, grabbing hold of the door handle.

Surprised, she turned to see Nick holding on the door handle. "What's wrong?"

"What's wrong?" he asked, incredulous. "You just cut off that lady back there!"

Paige frowned in confusion. "Huh?"

"Watch out!"

A car suddenly braked in front of her and she swerved to avoid him, squeezing in between a truck and an SUV in the next lane. They honked at her, but she ignored them. "I did not cut her off," she declared huffily.

Nick's breath hissed through his tightly clamped lips. "Yes, you did. Where the hell did you learn to drive anyway?"

Offended, she sniffed and switched lanes yet again. "I happen to be a good driver."

He eyed the speedometer. "Watch your speed," he gritted out.

"I'm within the speed limit," she shot back.

"You're going ninety!"

"I am?" She glanced at the instruments and rolled her eyes. He was such a cop. "I almost missed my exit!" With another burst of speed, she crossed all lanes of traffic and barely made the exit. Once on the surface street again, she slowed down and drove sedately.

"See? We're here, safe and sound." She flicked on the signal and turned into the parking lot in front of a bookstore. Pulling into a parking space, she dared to glance at him.

He was glaring at her. "Remind me never to let you drive."

"Nonsense," she dismissed with a sniff. "I'm a good driver. It's a crime not to take a car like this through its paces."

Nick gave her a sharp, assessing glance. A reluctant grin tugged at his lips. "Well, what do you know? Inside Dr. Paige Harrington lurks a daredevil."

No, not a daredevil. Just a woman who's decided to live her life for a change. She didn't say anything as she got out of the car. As soon as she walked through the doors, the crisp smell of new books surrounded her. She smiled. She'd always loved that smell. As a youngster, she'd hung around here, preferring to spend all of her free time between the pages of a good book. The manager of the bookstore knew her and Paige was counting on her help to escape.

She loitered in the romance section, picking up several books and pretending to read them. Nick was never far from her side, his face devoid of any reaction as he glanced at the racy covers of some of the books. Paige looked around surreptitiously, finally spotting the person she was looking for.

"Excuse me, I need to talk to the manager." Hurrying over to the counter, she explained in hushed tones what she needed and prayed her friend wouldn't ask too many questions. A minute later Paige smiled, now armed with vital escape route information.

She walked back to his side. "I need to go to the ladies' room," she announced. Her stomach sank in dismay as he followed her down the hall. "Please don't embarrass me by standing guard right outside the door. I'm only going over there." She pointed to the door at the end.

He looked undecided but gave in after a moment. "I'll be right here."

Paige stifled the joyous squeal of triumph that threatened to burst out. Managing to nod her head in agreement, she walked down the deserted hallway. But instead of going through the door marked Ladies, she made her way to the next door marked Private. Punching in the code that unlocked the door, she slipped inside. Heart beating overtime, she hurried through the maze of boxes until she reached a back door marked Exit. Palms damp with nervousness, she quickly made her way outside to where her car was parked and drove away.

Nick glanced at his watch. What the hell was taking Paige so long? She'd been in the ladies' room for over ten minutes now. He rapped on the door. "Paige? Are you all right?"

No answer.

Something was wrong. He turned the knob and pushed the door open. His gut told him she wasn't here but he looked inside the stalls anyway. Empty. Pushing past a woman who promptly shrieked at the sight of him, he ran out to the parking lot. Her car was gone.

He cursed soundly. Paige had given him the slip. *Wait 'til I get my hands around your pretty little neck.* When he found her, he was going to shackle the good doctor to his side. Gritting his teeth, he pulled out his cell phone and punched in some numbers. He had to find her right away.

* * * * *

Paige took a sip of her wine and made an effort to relax. Everything was fine. She didn't have to be so nervous. Of all the restaurants in the city, Nick would have a hard time finding her in this one. She refused to think of what would happen when she got home. She'll cross that bridge when she came to it.

"You seem a little quiet," Dan observed.

She flashed him a reassuring smile. "Am I?"

He took her hand in his. "I've been looking forward to tonight."

No sparks of electricity raced up her arm. Disappointment began to fill her. When Nick touched her, even briefly, she felt like she'd been hit by lightning. Why didn't she feel that way with Dan?

His voice lowered. "Would you like to come back to my place after dinner?"

This was it. He was inviting her to spend time with him alone. So why wasn't she thrilled? She gave Dan what she hoped was an inviting smile. "I'd love to."

He squeezed her hand and gave her an intimate look. She picked up her wine and sipped, hoping it would calm her down. *Don't think of Nick. Get in the moment with Dan,* she reminded herself. *Go with the flow.*

"Did you really think I wouldn't be able to find you?" a very pissed, very ominous masculine voice said over her head.

Paige choked. Her hand shook, forcing her to place the wineglass back on the table.

"Get up. We're going home." Nick spoke in measured tones, but she heard the throbbing anger underneath.

Dan looked at him askance. "Excuse me? Who are you?"

She squeezed his hand in warning. "Dan, let me explain."

Nick planted his body right next to her and took hold of her arm. "Let's go."

Dan stood up, ready to play the knight in shining armor. "Hey, buddy. I think you better let her go."

Paige looked up at Nick, wincing at the cold anger written all over his face. "Nick, I—"

"I don't want to hear it. If you know what's good for you, you'll get your ass up out of that chair and come with me."

With a frown, Dan threw her a puzzled look before confronting Nick. "I don't know what you think you're doing, but— Hey!"

Nick shoved him back in the chair. "Listen. This is none of your business. I would advise you to stay out of it."

Looking on in dismay, Paige grimaced as Dan bristled and stood up belligerently. "I'm going to have you thrown out of here," he declared.

Pulling out his badge, Nick pushed it in Dan's face. "Police business." He turned to Paige and gave her a mocking smile. "Would you like me to handcuff you in front of all these people?"

A look around confirmed that they were becoming a spectacle. Paige stood up and glanced apologetically at Dan. "I'm so sorry, Dan. I'll explain everything. I promise."

Nick pulled her along, his hold none too gentle. Poor Dan was left at the table, looking shell-shocked. Paige tripped, and gritted her teeth when he didn't even stop until they were outside.

"Will you slow down?" she hissed.

He turned to her, furious. "If I were you, I'd keep my mouth shut until we get to your apartment. At the moment, I'm not feeling too charitable toward you." There was a police cruiser waiting out in the parking lot. Nick waved at the officer sitting inside the car. "Thanks for the ride, Diaz. I can take over from here."

Diaz grinned. "Are you sure, Santorelli? You want me to hang around for a little bit?" At Nick's scowl, he held up his hands. "Just kidding. See ya later." He drove away, leaving them standing in the parking lot.

"How did you find me?" she finally asked.

"I got the information from your friend at the hospital." Nick held out his hand. "Give me the key to the car."

"Nick," she began.

"Give me the goddamn key," he growled.

Paige blinked and handed it to him. He unlocked her car. "Get in. And if you try anything, so help me, I'm going to paddle your ass and give you what you deserve."

She clamped her mouth shut and got in the car, wincing when he slammed the door before getting in the other side. She swallowed as she stole a look at his profile. He looked so forbidding. His face was like granite. Biting her lower lip, she clutched her purse in her hand. The silence was thick and filled with tension. Wanting to explain, she looked at him.

His glare was filled with warning, promising the retribution he would hand out later. She gulped and turned away. Didn't she deserve a chance to explain? She faced him again, opening her mouth to speak.

He only shook his head at her. Heaving a sigh, she turned to look out the window. She was starting to get mad. How dare he treat her like she was some recalcitrant child to be punished?

The scenery went by in a shapeless blur. Hah! And he said *she* drove fast. They were passing other cars like they were flying. She didn't even want to guess how fast he was going. She sat there, stewing and simmering, until he pulled into her building's parking garage. Without waiting for him to open her door, she got out and marched to the elevator. Head held high, she ignored him and all his seething macho anger until they strode into her apartment.

She was disconcerted to see him standing mere inches away from her. She took a step back. "Your behavior tonight was inexcusable. You had no right to treat me the way you did."

He stepped forward, anger lining every stiff muscle in his body. "Don't talk to me about inexcusable behavior. What you did was stupid and idiotic." He grabbed her arms. "Do you even know what could have happened to you because of that foolish stunt you pulled?"

Her chin lifted in defiance. "But *nothing* happened. This is all a waste of time. I'm not in any danger. Nobody is after me."

His brows drew together in a thunderous frown. "Of all the dim-witted things to say. How can you be so sure the killer doesn't know you, Paige? How do you know he's not already stalking you?" His grip tightened around her arms. "All he needs is a small window of opportunity to kill you."

"When I agreed to have somebody watch me, I told my father I had no intention of disrupting my life," she snapped back. "My whole life has been planned *for* me, Detective. From what school I went to, to what course of study I took. Now that I'm on my own, believe me, I value my freedom and independence too much to sit at home scared that this man will find me."

"You honestly believe that you're safe? Then why would your father make arrangements to have you watched?"

"Because he's an overprotective father with friends in high places," she shot back. "I have faith in your police department, and I've been assured they're working this case 'round the clock."

"Then you're not as smart as I thought, Doc," he countered in a mocking tone. He advanced on her. "What if you walk the two blocks home from the hospital, lost in thought, exhausted after a long shift, and a stranger creeps up behind you and gets you like this?"

In a flurry of movement, Nick hooked his arm around her neck. Paige only had time to gasp in surprise as she found herself subdued and unable to move. His breath feathered over her cheek as he spoke.

"He pulls you into an alley, where he pushes you against the wall and sticks a knife in your throat." His arms tightened around her. "That's what he did to that poor, unsuspecting woman, Paige. He pulled her behind some cars, brutally raped her and slit her throat." To emphasize his point, he drew an imaginary line across her neck.

Paige shivered, his words painting a vivid picture in her mind.

"Do you still want to take chances with your life?" he asked bluntly.

His arms loosened and let her go. Paige backed away from him. "Stop trying to scare me."

His eyes flashed with anger. "I'm trying to shock some sense into you. You've been sheltered all your life from the harsh realities of the streets. You don't even realize the enormity of the situation you're in. I have better things to do than watch over a spoiled princess like you."

Her eyes narrowed. Paige clenched her fists. "I'm not spoiled. I always longed for the day when nobody could tell me what to do or where I had to go, Detective. I don't want to go there again."

"The fact that you're the sole witness to a murder is not a joke. I want you to listen to me when I tell you that your life might very well be in danger. You need to be scared. Maybe you'll finally act with some sense." He grabbed her arm. "Don't ever do anything like that again. It's my job to protect you. I'm not playing games."

"It's a job to you but it's my *life*," she snapped. "I resent the fact that I can't even go out on a date because you're there watching me."

He shot her an incredulous look. "Is that what this is all about? A date?"

She glared at him in resentment. "You wouldn't understand."

"What's the matter, Doc?" he mocked. "Are you that horny? Been awhile, has it?"

Paige stiffened and gave him an angry shove. "Don't make fun of me."

Nick stopped her before she could escape to her bedroom. "What's going on, Paige?"

"Let me go," she hissed between gritted teeth.

"Not until you tell me the truth."

"You wouldn't understand," she repeated dully.

"Is sex really that important to you?"

Paige choked. This had to be the most humiliating moment of her life. "You don't know what you're talking about."

"Then what is it?"

Oh, to hell with it. He wanted to know, didn't he? "I'm not like you, Nick. I haven't had a normal life. I didn't have a normal childhood." She avoided his eyes. "I was a very smart kid. As a result, I was way ahead of my class. I was sixteen when I graduated from college. I've only had one boyfriend and had sex twice." She gave a self-deprecating laugh. "So you see, you're talking to a freak of nature. It took me a long time to earn my independence. And even longer to admit that my life was lonely and boring compared to other women my age. So I decided I'm going to enjoy my life."

"Hence the car," he concluded quietly.

She gave a tight nod. "Hence the car. I've also decided to see what sex is all about. The two times I had sex were forgettable. I didn't enjoy it." She choked on the words but forged on, "As a doctor, I have clinical knowledge about sex. But as a healthy young woman, I know next to nothing about it. I decided it was time to learn."

"And you picked this *Dan* to teach you?" he asked, unable to keep the disbelief out of his voice.

She lifted her chin. "Why not? He's a gentleman. I figured he'd be willing to teach a twenty-six-year-old the joys of sex."

A flush covered Nick's high cheekbones. "Paige…"

Not wanting to see the pity in his eyes, she turned away. "So there it is, the reason why I felt compelled to escape. I was horrified by the tragedy of the murder I witnessed. And I'll cooperate with the police and my father as much as I can. But I'll be damned if my life will be put on hold. All my life I've done what others have wanted me to do. I think it's time I start doing what *I* want to do." Now that she'd vented, she felt deflated somehow. "I hope you're happy, now that you've found out exactly how sad and boring my life is. I apologize for tricking you the way I did. But I refuse to apologize for wanting to go on with my life."

She turned away and walked to her bedroom, carefully closing the door behind her. Tears pricked at the corners of her eyes. Muttering under her breath about the unfairness of the world, she toed off her chunky-heeled pumps. She pulled the dress over her head and threw it into the hamper in a fit of rage. Walking to her dresser, she unclasped the single strand of her mother's pearls at her neck and tossed it on the polished top. Next, she attacked the pins holding her hair up and began brushing her hair with merciless tugs, wincing at the pain in her scalp.

To her horror, the brush flew from her hand and skidded across the polished top of the dresser, knocking a bottle of perfume over. The bottle fell over the side and landed on the hardwood floor, crashing into a thousand tiny pieces.

Her bedroom door crashed against the wall. Nick rushed in, his gun in hand. Paige gaped at him, unable to move.

Nick froze. He stared at her, standing amidst broken glass and barely dressed in a low-cut silk bra and matching thong. "What the hell happened?" he rasped. He couldn't take his gaze off her.

Paige felt his eyes like a physical caress. The shattered glass lay forgotten. The enticing, sensual scent of the perfume rose between them. She knew she should at least cover herself, but the fire in his eyes rooted her to the spot. Heat seeped through her skin. She felt hot. So hot. She finally summoned the energy to bring an arm up to cover her breasts.

"Don't move," he commanded in a hoarse voice. He flicked the safety on his gun and stuck it in the back of his jeans. He made his way over to her, carefully pushing the broken shards of glass to the side. "Are you hurt?"

She couldn't speak for the huge lump in her throat, so she simply shook her head. There was such heat in his eyes, heat that called an answering firestorm deep inside her. The intensity of it made her knees weak.

"Goddammit, Paige, you scared the hell out of me." His hands curved around her waist as he lifted her clear of the sharp glass and deposited her on the other side of the bed.

God, why were his hands so hot on her skin? "It was an accident," she began to explain. Her breath hitched in her throat at the way he was staring at her.

Following the direction of his gaze, Paige flushed even deeper when she saw how the mounds of her too-generous breasts jutted against the cups of the bra. And was that a nipple peeking through the top? She pushed away from him, her eyes darting around for something within reach so she could cover herself.

He stilled her movements. "I can't figure you out." A blunt finger came up and traced her damp lower lip.

Her pulse skittered out of control. She couldn't look away from his dark eyes. "W-what do you mean?"

Nick shifted closer. He was so close that she felt the tremendous heat coming off him in waves. "I can't figure out why a beautiful woman like you would choose to hide under shapeless clothing."

She looked away. His hand gently nudged her chin to turn her face back to him. Her lashes lowered.

He bent his head, his cheek rubbing against hers in a tender, sensuous movement. "I grew up with four sisters. I remember them spending hours and hours trying on new clothes, makeup and hairstyles. They wanted to look beautiful." His finger skimmed over her cheek. "You, however, do the exact opposite. You put your hair in a ponytail, wear eyeglasses that I doubt you really need, and live in jeans and sweatshirts."

She squirmed. Her nipples were tight, painful points pushing against her bra. Unfamiliar warmth began to spread from her lower belly. "Nick," she breathed. What was he doing?

He traced the madly beating pulse at the base of her throat. "Tell me why."

How could she think when he touched her like that? She moaned. At the sound, he bent and brushed his lips against hers. A shudder tore through her as their bodies came into contact. His skin was rough where hers was smooth. She could feel a disturbing length of stiff flesh touching her bare skin.

He plunged his fingers into her hair and tilted her face up. Licking the corner of her lips, he bade her to open her mouth. "Give me your tongue, Paige. Let me taste you."

Her lips parted. Her heartbeat thundered in her ears. She touched her tongue to his, shyly, hesitantly. She jumped when a sound rumbled from his lips. "Nick?"

"Do it again," he ordered gruffly.

"This?" she asked, touching her tongue to his. He emitted a sound between a groan and a growl before he took over and pushed inside her mouth.

She moaned. Her limbs felt heavy and weightless. His hands splayed on her back, pulling her closer and keeping her there. Her senses whirled. Their lips parted and clung together again and again. She was breathing hard when he eventually let her up for air.

"You don't even know what it does to me to see you like this," he whispered, his voice rough.

She shivered. "I need to cover up," she whispered.

He tightened his arms around her. "Why?" he asked hoarsely. "Why do you cover up with shapeless clothing?"

She bit her lip. Paige recognized the slow, syrupy feeling that invaded her bones as sexual arousal. With something close to wonder, she realized he was just as affected, judging by the thick length of steel that was pushing against the front of his jeans. Her nipples hardened into tight little points, and somewhere in her pussy an ache began to grow.

The warm cocoon of his arms almost muffled her words. "I was just a kid when I entered medical school." Nick leaned closer to catch her words. "I had a hard time adjusting." She took a deep breath. "I hated the attention. I felt like a freak of nature. I wanted to be taken seriously."

"By hiding the way you look?" he asked against her hair.

Paige nodded tightly. "I made myself look as plain as I could. No makeup, loose clothing, the works. I even took to wearing glasses, even though I'd always worn contact lenses."

"What happened?" he asked, his lips sounding close to her ear.

She tried to smile but failed. "It worked. Too well, I think. I didn't date at all through medical school. I was too busy studying."

"And after?"

Her slim shoulders shrugged. "I saw no reason to change. When I started working at the hospital, I wanted to prove myself. None of the other doctors thought a twenty-something trauma surgeon could do her job well."

"They're all fools if they're unable to see that you can. You shouldn't let them dictate your life, Paige."

"I realize that. But my work is very important to me. I want them to look beyond the face and see that I'm a damn good doctor."

He pushed her soft hair away from her face. "You're a beautiful, sexy woman, Paige, as well as one hell of a doctor."

She began to shake with the force of the feelings coursing through her. "Nick." She didn't know what she wanted, she just knew she wanted something.

"Yeah?" he whispered against her ear. He cupped her buttocks and pulled her up against him.

A small whimper was all she could utter.

He was kneading her ass in slow, sensuous movements. Moisture flooded her pussy, soaking through her underwear.

"It's a crime to cover this up, Paige. You should be proud of how sexy you are." He nuzzled the thick tumble of curls at her shoulder. "You should always wear your hair down like this."

A dark flush covered her face. The look in Nick's eyes was unmistakably arousal. As a doctor, she'd studied human sexuality at length. But studying it and feeling it were two entirely different things. For the first time in her life, she felt instantly and unbearably aroused.

Her nipples pushed against the silk of her bra, the material scraping the sensitive tips. Paige barely resisted the urge to rub them to give herself some relief. She was filled with heady, unfamiliar feelings.

She knew she should cover herself, but there was something thrilling and forbidden about the way Nick Santorelli was looking at her. His hot gaze speared her body, igniting an answering flame deep within her.

Oh God, she wanted this man.

Paige bit her lip as fresh moisture flooded through her. Her ex-boyfriend, Jeff, had never aroused these feelings in her, never sent her blood racing like wildfire through her veins. Her thought process was seriously impaired. Her body, on the other hand, was having no such problem, coming alive at his touch.

His hands rubbed her soft skin. "Paige," he murmured. His fingers traced the soft material that disappeared into a thin line snuggled between the cheeks of her ass. His hands passed over her buttocks, cupping the firm, tight mounds.

For the first time in her life, Paige wanted to be touched all over. Restlessly, she rubbed her breasts against the cotton of his shirt. She moaned softly.

His hands tightened on her ass before moving up her back, deftly unhooking the clasp of her bra. No words were exchanged. Thick silence filled the room.

Paige lowered her arms. The bra fell to the floor.

Nick glanced down at her bare breasts, his eyes darkening. "You're perfect. Round and generously curved, tipped with pale, sweet nipples."

The look in his eyes hypnotized Paige. Never had a man looked at her in such a hungry way. Her breasts felt heavy and ultra-sensitive.

"Nick," she whimpered, softly pleading.

He cupped her breast, the soft flesh fitting his large hand perfectly. Nick brushed the nipple with his thumb. Paige gasped at the delicious sensations that shot through her womb. He did it again and again.

Paige bit her lip and closed her eyes. Her pussy flooded, the wetness seeping through her thong.

Nick pinched her nipple, the sharp sting followed by hot pleasure.

Paige shuddered.

"You're unbelievably beautiful," he whispered hoarsely. "I have to—"

He lifted her flesh and drew her nipple into his mouth and sucked. In that moment, Paige was catapulted into a place she had never known before. The sensation of his mouth pulling at her breast was the most erotic thing she had ever felt, and she never wanted him to stop. Every pull of his mouth elicited an answering tug in her pussy, making her ache deep within.

She looked down, seeing her breast in his mouth, her nipple captured between his lips. It felt surreal. Nick Santorelli, gorgeous detective, was enthusiastically sucking, tugging and licking her. The little noises he was making against her flesh triggered a deep well of longing within her.

He gently bit down. Paige moaned.

At the sound, he straightened and captured her mouth in a heated kiss. She was helpless in the face of the sensual forces attacking her, opening instantly to his insistent tongue. Nick Santorelli was a masterful kisser. He drew her responses at an alarming rate. She was dizzy from the pleasure swimming through her.

He led her back to the bed and gently followed her down, his legs easing her thighs apart. As he lay on top of her, Nick rotated his hips slowly over her heated core.

Paige jerked against him with a gasp. "Oh, God!"

"Easy." He pushed her arms up over her head, and held them with his hand, shifting sideways on the bed.

Though she was almost naked, Paige felt no fear or trepidation. No embarrassment. Instead, she felt proud of her body. He made her feel proud by the hunger in his eyes alone. She felt sexy and desirable. She glanced at his dark head between her breasts. *This gorgeous man wanted her!*

"I can't stop touching you," he murmured against her navel.

Her muscles contracted at his touch, shivers racking her body as he licked his way lower. Paige strained against his grip, but he wasn't budging. She writhed and twisted on the bed, arching her lower body up to him.

He slid back up to her breast and flicked at her engorged nipple. He lapped at the tip, leaving it moist. Her breathing quickened, her chest moving up and down, pushing more of her flesh into his mouth.

Nick pulled the stiff crest between his teeth and gently bit down.

She could only whimper.

"Delicious," he grunted, before sucking the entire areola into the hot depths of his mouth.

Paige moaned, protesting against not being able to move, but he wouldn't let her go. With his free hand, he glided down her body to her aching mound. In a move that took her by surprise, he pulled the silk taut against her flesh. Her labia puffed out, her clitoris caught in the tight cloth. Her eyes opened wide.

"You don't know how gorgeous your pussy looks to me like this." His piercing gaze found hers. "Keep your hands right where they are."

He waited for her brief nod before he let her go and slid down her length. Her clitoris was a prominent bump against the damp silk, and he flicked at it with the tip of his finger.

Sparks spread from the brief contact to every nerve ending in her body.

"Feel that?" he asked roughly.

"Yes," she whispered.

"You smell like a woman aroused." He traced the wet spot on the crotch of her thong. "You're soaked through." Shouldering her legs wider apart, he suddenly bent and licked repeatedly at her clit.

"Ohhh," she gasped. Tingles raced up and down her spine, spreading outward to her legs, down to her toes. Pleasure bombarded her starved senses, and filled her to overflowing. She moaned, long and low, and pleaded for she knew not what. Through the silk, he laved her, the delicious rasp of his tongue pushing the material against her flesh. The friction drove her crazy. "I-I can't—"

He hummed against her clit before he bit down, gently.

"Yes, yes," she chanted mindlessly.

"Come for me, Paige," he ordered. "Right now." He sucked firmly. Stars exploded in the backs of her eyes. A wave of intense pleasure slammed into her, robbing her of breath. It took possession of her senses, depriving her of control. She didn't know it, but she was chanting Nick's name as she fell headlong into her orgasm. Tremors worked their way through her writhing body. By the time the tumult was over, she was boneless and weak, replete with satisfaction. Her eyes drifted open to find Nick looking down at her. Bringing a hand up to cup his cheek, she whispered, "Thank you."

Nick turned his face into her palm and licked her soft skin. "For what?"

She smiled. "My very first orgasm."

His dark eyes narrowed. "You've never had an orgasm?"

"You know, this conversation could be highly embarrassing, if you think about it," she commented lightly, trying to remain casual about a sore subject. Paige rubbed against the cock that was pushing insistently against her stomach.

He gripped her waist. "Not even once?"

"No, not even once," she assured him in a soft voice. "I can't explain to you how it felt, Nick. It was…amazing. Unbelievable."

His hands held her steady. "I can't believe you've only had one boyfriend."

She toyed with his shirt and tugged it from his waistband. She didn't stop until she encountered warm, bare skin. "Don't forget that I was years younger than everybody I went to school with. And by the time I reached dating age, I was too immersed in studying to give it much thought. And with Jeff, well," she trailed off, feeling embarrassed. "He was concerned more for his pleasure, really, than mine. Then I just lost interest, it wasn't very enjoyable."

Nick dropped his forehead on her shoulder. "Jeez."

She nuzzled his hair, enjoying the soft, thick texture. "What? It was great. I'd love to feel it again," she added in a shy voice.

The look in his eyes was tortured when he pulled back. "Oh, man. I can't do this."

"Why not?" Paige couldn't believe her daring, but she had to be honest. She wanted to come again. She wanted to feel the sharp tingling that spread from her toes up to her thighs and the glorious explosion of pleasure that shook her body. She wanted to feel it again and again. With him.

"I shouldn't do this," he muttered.

"Nick?" A sick feeling began to swirl in her stomach. The same old feelings of insecurity, inadequacy that she'd thought she'd gotten over, came rushing back.

Tenderly, he drew her hair back from her face. "I can't do this, Paige. I don't want to hurt you."

"Hurt me how?" She stiffened, every muscle in her body bracing for the rejection she knew was to come.

"I'm afraid that you'd feel an emotional commitment if we do this." He touched a finger to her lips when she would have spoken. "Because you're so inexperienced. I don't want you mistaking sexual attraction for more than what it is."

Paige looked at him in earnest. "I wouldn't—"

"Paige, sex for women is different," he began gently. "To a man, sex is a physical function, a release." A slight grimace twisted his lips. "Sad but true. I'm not the one to give you the experience you want."

The hurt in her chest blossomed. "Why not you, Nick?"

"You need somebody gentle, somebody who'd treat you the way you deserve to be treated."

"And you can't?" she argued, though inside she was breaking.

"I've done things that would shock you."

Her brow lifted in challenge. "I'm a doctor, remember? I've studied human anatomy exhaustively. Nothing will shock me."

"The clinical part, yes," Nick replied. "But you haven't done half the things I've done, or the things that I'd expect you to do."

In spite of the hurt she was feeling, heat was spreading through her at his words. She swallowed. "What things?"

Nick closed his eyes. "Things that would shock some people, Paige. Different positions, different acts. I'd expect you to do them, enjoy them, not just once, but many, many times. Frequently."

Her pussy flooded at his words, despite the hurt she was feeling. "And you think I can't do it? Don't sugarcoat it, Nick. If you regret what we just did, because it was just an impulse, then say so. Don't lie to me."

He gripped her arms tightly. "I'm not sugarcoating it. I don't have to. What if I were to tell you that I love your breasts and I'd love to see your nipples pierced?"

Her eyes widened in shock.

"That's what I mean, Paige," he growled roughly. "Vanilla sex is not for me. What if I told you I love your clit, and how it stands out like a little button that's just begging to be pierced, too? Would you do that for me?" His voice roughened, deepened. "I like to talk when I'm fucking, I want to be able to tell you what I'm feeling, what I want to do to you. And I won't use nice words."

Paige swallowed.

"I'll say I want to fuck you, long and deep, until you scream. I want to fuck your throat. I want to watch you swallow my cock so deep, until I come and you take all of it. All of me," he emphasized. "And I'd love to fuck your ass."

She stared at him, unable to say a word.

"Now do you realize why I'm not the one for you? I can't do that to you, Paige. You need to learn first, to enjoy yourself, to meet other people. You're too pure for me." He gave her a regretful, rueful smile. "Would you even have the guts to ask me to fuck you?"

She opened her mouth, but stopped when he shook his head.

"I want to hear you say *fuck my pussy, eat me, lick me.* Can you say those words? Words people consider dirty?" He stared deep into her eyes. "Would you trust me to tie you up and spank you? Do whatever I want with you?"

"Teach me, Nick."

He froze.

"Teach me. Show me all the things that you were talking about. Show me how t-to put your cock in my mouth. I want to swallow. Teach me how good sex can be. I don't want vanilla sex. I want *your* kind of sex."

Nick shook his head. "You don't know what you're asking for."

Her hands twined around his neck. "Yes, I do. I'd let you do all those things to me, Nick. Whatever you want. Just teach me."

He tried to pull her arms down. "Paige—"

"Would it be so hard to make yourself teach me? When you pulled on my nipples, I felt it here." She grabbed his hand and pushed it down to her pussy. "Teach me. I'll do anything. I'll even learn to say dirty words."

His fingers curved around her mound. "No," was what he said, but his fingers sought and rubbed her clit.

"Yes, just like that," she moaned. "I want you to teach me to enjoy my body the way a woman is meant to." She nuzzled the side of his neck, licking his salty skin. "I want to do all the things you said, Nick. I want to do them with you."

"Jesus." Nick heaved his body off of hers with a jerk. "I shouldn't have done this. I wasn't thinking. All I could think of when I saw you was—" he took a deep breath "—It doesn't matter. I'm here to protect you, not corrupt you. I can't do what you're asking, Paige. I just can't."

Paige turned her head away, stung by his rejection.

"Paige? Look at me."

"Please," she whispered. "Just go."

For the longest time, he just looked at her. She stubbornly refused to look up at him. He sighed and pushed himself off her. "I'll get something to clean up the broken glass. I'll be right back."

She could feel him staring down at her but she refused to meet his gaze. Paige held her breath until he walked away and pulled the door closed behind him. Then she stood up and locked her door. Even through the deep breath she took, the hurt pierced through. She carefully gathered the shards of glass and pushed them in one corner. Paige lay down on the bed and curled into a little ball, closing her eyes tightly. Nothing had changed. She'd always found herself in situations where she wasn't suited or didn't belong. All her life she'd had to fight first impressions, overcome judgments. She was always the outsider looking in. With Nick's words, she once again felt like she was a kid trying to grow up too soon. The rejection hurt.

She looked down at her reddened nipple, the flesh swollen and aching from his kisses. With a finger, she traced the little love bite he had given her. She, Paige Harrington, who had been accused of being frigid, had gone up in flames within seconds of being touched by Nick Santorelli.

In the course of her young life, she had given up thinking of herself as a sexual creature. The first time she'd had sex had been a horrible experience, hurried and unfeeling, completely forgettable. Naïve as she had been, she thought it was completely natural for her not to enjoy herself. The second time had been just as disastrous. Jeff had been concerned primarily with his pleasure. Her face grimaced in distaste at the memory. He had pumped into her, grunted a few times, and then gave a great heave. Seconds later, it was over. She didn't feel a thing.

Nick Santorelli was a different matter.

In his arms, she'd been rendered senseless. Her hand went to her pussy, her fingers immediately awash in wetness. He had effortlessly aroused her, quickly and totally. For years, Paige had looked at other people and wondered if sex was really all that it was cracked up to be. But now that she had a taste of what it was really like to feel the blood coursing hotly through her veins, she was hooked. She wanted more of that feeling. But Nick didn't want her.

Seeing her naked had aroused him, yes, but not enough to overcome his reluctance. He simply didn't feel the same way she did. Paige hugged her pillow tight. The knock at her door came a couple of minutes later, but she ignored it.

"Paige." The door muffled his voice.

She didn't answer, hoping he would just get the message and leave. He called her name again. Then silence. After a few moments, she heard footsteps moving away from the door. He'd given up.

Chapter Four

The next day, an uneasy truce hung between them. Paige had rebuffed Nick's attempts at conversation. Lucky for her, he didn't force the issue. When he announced that he had an appointment he couldn't miss and politely asked her to go, she reluctantly agreed. He'd already said he wasn't leaving her anyway, so that really didn't give her any choice. She sat stiffly in the car, grateful for the music which filled the thick silence that surrounded them.

Only when he pulled up in front of a sprawling bungalow on a tree-lined street did she look at him curiously. The lawn was lush and neatly kept. Colorful flowers and box hedges created borders on each side of the brick walkway. An intricately detailed wrought iron fence surrounded the property. "Where are we?"

"I hope you don't mind. This is my parents' house. We have a traditional Sunday get-together for our family." He managed to look sheepish. "I've been warned that if I don't make an appearance, Mom will disown me." When she remained silent, he went on. "I understand if you don't want to stay. Let me just show my face and I'll make our excuses."

Just then, a couple of kids peeked out the front door and shrieked, "It's Uncle Nick!"

Her heart softened. "It's all right. I don't mind."

Nick gave her a smile and got out of the car in time to hug the kids that ran out to meet him. Paige followed them into the house, and endured the curious looks the kids threw her. Pausing under an archway that led to the family room, she stood, bemused.

It was loud and chaotic. She loved it.

Two comfortable chintz sofas rested against walls that were painted butter yellow. Light, gauzy drapes billowed gently against the open windows. A big-screen TV sat in one corner. On top of the fireplace mantel hung a large family portrait. Framed photographs took up every available space, all of them with smiling faces. The house had a cozy, lived-in look. Paige absorbed everything at once. Everybody was talking at the same time, and kids were running around laughing and giggling.

Nick's mother stood in the middle of it all, clucking at the antics of her grandchildren, but clearly loving it. When Nick introduced Paige, Angela Santorelli pulled her into a warm, effusive hug. "I apologize, Paige. My grandchildren know better than to run around, but here at Grandma's house, they're free to do anything," she said with an indulgent smile. "Come, come. I want you to meet everybody."

By turns, she was introduced to Nick's brothers and sisters. There was Anthony, a prosecutor in the DA's office, and his wife, Grace, with their twin sons Michael and Marcus. Anthony was tall, and wore wire-rimmed glasses. "I've heard of your father, Paige. He was a legend in his own time."

Paige murmured her reply, turning to face Jason, the other brother, who was a firefighter. He had light brown hair and a crooked smile. *Ah,* she thought. *This one's clearly a ladies' man.* The oldest of the girls, Patricia, worked as a teacher and was the mother of little Nicky and Raffy. Her husband, Gino, was a fellow teacher. Nina was a reporter for the local paper. And the youngest, Rebecca, was still in college. They all bore the stamp of a Santorelli, with twinkling dark eyes, contagious grins and gorgeous Italian good looks. Nick's father came forward, enveloping her in a bear hug. *So this is what Nick's going to look like forty years from now.*

Joseph Santorelli was still handsome, with thick salt-and-pepper hair, cut military-short. His face was lined with laugh lines, his eyes wise and dark. He shook her hand and said a booming voice, "Welcome to our home, Paige. As you can see, my children have absolutely no regard for propriety." His eyes twinkled as he caught one of his grandchildren and hefted her up in his arms. "And the little ones, hah! They run circles around Angela and me, giving us headaches." But he said it with a smile and nuzzled the neck of the little girl.

Paige was struck by the obvious affection they all had for each other. There was good-natured ribbing, jokes, and above all, a love for the children. Accepting a cold soda from Nick, she moved off to the side and just...watched. For an only child who'd grown up with the perpetual silence of an empty house, this chaotic *fun* was an amazing sight. The TV was tuned to a basketball game, and although the men would glance occasionally at the screen, nobody was sitting on the couch.

The little girl, Raffy, came running up to her. Paige knelt down to her height. "Hello."

Raffy gave her a gap-toothed smile. "Your hair is pretty."

Her hand came up to touch the ponytail. "Thank you, Raffy."

"I like the color," she added, reaching out to finger a tendril of Paige's hair.

Nick sauntered over and scooped Raffy up in his arms. "What are you up to now, squirt?"

Raffy giggled with obvious adoration. "I like her hair, Uncle Nick."

Nick turned to Paige. "So do I."

She avoided his eyes, and focused on the little girl instead. "I like your hair, too, Raffy. Very nice."

The little girl wrinkled her nose. "I don't like my name."

Paige frowned. "You don't?"

Raffy shook her head. "My name is Rafaella. Uncle Nick said I was named after one of the Te-Teenage Mutant Ninja Turtles and that my Dad wore the costume and then my Mom fell in love with him—"

"O-kay," Nick interrupted with a laugh.

Patricia came up to them and caught the last part of what her daughter said. "Raffy, honey, I told you not to listen to Uncle Nick. Yours is a beautiful Italian name, sweetheart." With a smiling glance at Nick, she turned to Paige. "Nick has what we call Middle Child Syndrome."

His other siblings heard and laughed. This started another round of good-natured teasing. Paige enjoyed their lighthearted banter, and found herself laughing at some of the more outrageous childhood stories they told.

The only dim point was when she wandered over to the wall filled with family pictures. In the center was a large, framed photographed of a young woman who bore the unmistakable stamp of the Santorelli looks.

"My sister, Cecilia. She was killed last year." Nick had followed her, and stood over her shoulder. Although his voice was even, there was a wealth of sadness in it.

"Oh Nick, I'm sorry."

He shrugged. "It was a difficult time for all of us, especially Mom and Dad. Cecilia was very young, only a year older than Rebecca."

It was hard to imagine this warm, boisterous family hit with such a tragedy. "What happened?"

"She was stabbed in her apartment. The case is still open." His tone hardened with determination. "I swore that I would find the bastard that did it. That's the least I could do for her. But what few leads we had were dead ends." He glanced back at his family. The love and affection, as well as the protective instincts he felt for them was evident in his eyes. "It's been hard for my family. We're all looking for closure."

At that moment, Angela came out of the kitchen and announced, "Food's ready."

The brief moment was broken. With a hand at her elbow, Nick followed the rest of the family as they all trooped into the dining room. The Santorelli children took turns going to the kitchen and coming out with a platter. It struck her again how it looked like so much fun to be part of a large family.

Heaping plates of pasta and meat sauce filled the table. The mouthwatering smell of freshly baked garlic bread wafted in the air. A large bowl of salad was passed around, tossed with a dressing that Mrs. Santorelli made herself. The children had fried chicken as a special treat, and ate with a heartiness that was endearing.

"I'm so happy to see you here, Nick," his mother declared over the din of conversation. "I had just about given up hope that you would make it here today."

His siblings snickered. Nick shot them a glare before giving his mother a sheepish look. "I'm sorry, Mom. I've been so busy lately, but you know I come whenever I can."

"Of course, your absence has nothing to do with Carmen Mendoza across the street, right, Nicky?" Rebecca piped in, a naughty gleam in her eye.

Anthony choked and gulped down some water. Jason raised his eyes heavenward and clasped his hands on his chest. "Carmen. Of the curvy body and great a—"

"Jason!" Mrs. Santorelli froze her son with a disapproving stare.

Nina and Rebecca were trying hard to hide their smiles behind their white linen napkins. Patricia elbowed her smiling husband, who quickly wiped the grin off his face.

Carmen Mendoza. Of the curvy body and great ass, Paige thought, mentally finishing Jason's sentence. The delicious pasta turned to sawdust in Paige's mouth. She kept on chewing with mechanical precision, trying without success to regain the appetite she'd lost all of a sudden. *Carmen's probably tall and proportioned right, with endless legs to go with that great ass,* she thought sourly.

"Sorry, Mom," Jason offered before turning to Nick. "It's true, bro. She waits around for you to show up. That's why her curtain always twitches when you're around."

Nick glanced at Paige briefly before giving Jason a look full of brotherly retribution. "I haven't been around lately, so I don't know what you're talking about."

The enjoyment Paige had felt at being part of a happy family gathering evaporated. She concentrated on her food, trying to keep a blank face. *No wonder Nick didn't want her.* How could she even hope to compete with somebody like Carmen Mendoza? Paige could imagine what she looked like. Long, curly black hair, voluptuous body, long legs and of course, that great ass.

Nick leaned back and surveyed everybody seated around the table. "I miss a couple of Sunday get-togethers and everybody picks on me. Nobody's asked Jason about the redhead that's been seen hanging around the station lately."

"Which one?" Patricia asked, shaking her head and sharing a conspiratorial smile with the other women.

Mrs. Santorelli sighed. "Oh, Jason. When will you settle down with one woman? This playing around is not good. Not good at all."

Nick grinned. Jason squirmed in his chair. "I'm still young, Mom."

Joseph patted his wife's hand. "He'll settle when he's ready, Angie. Don't worry so."

Paige pushed her food around and around her plate, freezing when Nina spoke to her. "Ignore them, Paige. We're so used to girls chasing after our brothers, it's gotten tiresome." She rolled her eyes. "It was worse when we were going to school. I can't tell you how many girls wanted to be our friends so they could get close to our brothers."

Paige wasn't surprised. She nodded, having no idea how to respond to that.

"So, Paige, you never did tell us how you met Nick," Rebecca asked, a sly smile on her face.

"I, uh…we, uh," she stammered.

"Paige and I are working together on a case," Nick answered, bailing her out.

Nina looked at Paige, then back to Nick again. Her gaze was sharp. "What are you not telling us?"

All conversation ceased, and heads swung Nick's way.

Nick kept a straight face. "What?"

Anthony grinned. "Sorry, bro. I guess everybody knows when you're lying."

Joseph's steely-eyed gaze landed on his son's face. "I still have friends in the police department, Son."

Nick's expression was pained. He knew when he was cornered. "I've been assigned to watch over Paige."

Jason burst out laughing. "What did you do now? You must have pissed off somebody pretty high up, bro."

"Jason," Angela chided. She gave Paige a concerned look. "You're not in any trouble, are you, Paige?"

"Uh, no. Not really," she replied. She had no idea what to say or how much to reveal.

Nick once again helped her out. "Paige is an important witness to a big case."

Anthony's curiosity was piqued. "Which case?"

Nick hesitated a fraction of a second. "The mall murder."

All at once, everybody started commiserating with Paige and offering words of encouragement. Angela stood up and enveloped her in a warm, motherly hug. "With Nicky watching you, everything will be okay. I believe that."

A warm feeling filled Paige. They were so open and welcoming. They made her feel like she belonged, like she was part of a loving circle of a big family. A soft "thank you" was all she could say. As the meal progressed, she felt more and more involved. Grace revealed she was pregnant, and another round of hugs ensued. The men clapped Anthony on the back, exchanging knowing grins that only men understood. She felt Nick's eyes on her on more than one occasion, but she stubbornly refused to look at him.

The meal wound down, and Paige volunteered to help do the dishes. Her stomach sank when Nick announced he was helping too. Together, they stacked the dishes in the sink. Paige plunged her hands in the warm, soapy water, trying to ignore the big, gorgeous man next to her.

"You've been pretty quiet," he observed.

"It's fun. I've never been to a big family dinner before." She gave him a polite smile. "Thank you for bringing me."

"You're welcome. Now tell me what's bugging you."

Paige concentrated on scrubbing stubborn pasta sauce off a plate. "I don't know what you mean."

Nick faced her. "Tell me what's wrong."

Why not? The new Paige would tackle the issue head-on. The old Paige was the quiet, shy one. "I've been thinking. What happened between us last night— "

"Paige— "

"No, let me finish. When I— " she inhaled deeply, " — When I asked you to teach me, I put you in an uncomfortable position. I didn't mean to do that. I realize that it made things complicated and uncomfortable between us. Also, I didn't take into account that you have a life outside your job. I'm sorry."

"What the hell are you talking about?" he asked, irritated.

"I didn't stop to think that you might be involved with somebody." At his frown, she clarified, "Carmen Mendoza."

His eyes narrowed. "And you think the reason I said no is because of her?"

Paige picked up a plate and soaped it. "What else?"

Nick wiped his hands and shifted to stand behind her. Her breath stuck in her throat when his arms came around her, caging her against the sink.

"I've known Carmen Mendoza since we were in high school." He spoke against her hair. A thick knot of desire began to unfurl in the pit of her stomach. "If I wanted to, I would have taken her up on her offer a long time ago."

"Still," she insisted, striving for a cool voice. "It was wrong of me to just assume that you felt the same way."

He moved closer, his front touching her back. His arms tightened around her. "I did." His big hands splayed over her front. "I do."

Her mouth went dry. She froze.

"I had a hell of a time keeping my hands off you, Paige." He bent and nuzzled that sensitive spot below her ear. Her stomach dipped. "Right now, it's all I can do to stop myself from unbuttoning this blouse and seeing your perfect breasts again." His fingers began to undo the buttons that ran down her front. "Like this."

"Nick, what are you doing?" she hissed, getting all hot and bothered.

"Let me," he whispered back. "I've wanted to do this all afternoon. It's been driving me nuts imagining what kind of bra you have on. I pictured something red and sinful." He parted the sides of her blouse, revealing her lacy bra. His fingers ran lightly over her skin.

Her muscles contracted at the fleeting touch. Her breath got trapped in her lungs. She couldn't move at all.

"Instead, I find you wearing this demure white lace that can barely contain your breasts." He slipped under the cup, seeking and finding. "You're such a contradiction. Prim and proper on the outside, but sexy as hell inside."

He pushed her bra up and out of the way, cupping her in his hand. Paige whimpered. His thumb brushed her distended nipple, once, twice. A strangled moan escaped her lips.

"You're beautiful, Paige. And so sexy you drive me crazy." His other hand insinuated itself inside the waistband of her pants, under her bikini, heading straight down her abdomen, honing in on her pussy.

Paige bucked. But held tightly in his arms, she couldn't dislodge his hands.

"Oh God, Nick." She turned her face to his. "Don't do this."

A dark flush colored his cheekbones. "I have to. I can't stop myself, Paige."

His fingers plunged inside her moist heat. Her knees turned to jelly, and she could only clutch his arms for support.

"So hot. So wet." His lips sought hers. Paige was helpless to stop him. Her mouth opened under his. Just like that, common sense fled and she was a willing participant. His damp tongue delved into her mouth, pulling her deeper into an erotic duel.

He cupped her mound. "Wider," he rasped.

It never occurred to her not to obey him. Her legs opened wider. He parted the folds of her pussy and insinuated his fingers in the wet depths. "Does this feel like I don't feel the same way?" he rasped in her ear, pushing his erection against her ass. "My cock is killing me, Paige. I sat across the table the whole meal, thinking I'd like to tear off this demure blouse you're wearing and get at what's underneath."

He licked her ear. She moaned softly. Nick captured her nipple between thumb and forefinger, pinching it just hard enough to send a modicum of pain streaking through her. But the pleasure that followed the pain turned her gasp into a whimper.

She arched her back, pushing more of her flesh into his hand. Assaulted on two fronts, Paige could only respond to the push and pull of his fingers.

"Do you like that?" he asked, his voice hoarse and almost unrecognizable. "Do you like my fingers in your pussy, Paige?"

"Nick," Paige moaned.

"Do you?" He pushed deeper, learning the secret folds and hollows, delving into her willing pussy.

"Yes," she breathed.

The door swung open. Paige froze, horrified. "*Nick,*" she hissed in desperation.

Nick shifted to shield her, his arms tightening around her sides.

"Nick?" His mother stood hovering at the kitchen door.

Paige lowered her face, mortified. *Oh God, what had she been thinking*?

"Can you give us a minute, Mom?" Nick's voice was strangled, and he spoke without looking at his mother.

After a moment of silence, Angela backed out of the doorway. "Come on, girls. It looks like they've got everything under control. We should leave them to it."

Paige heard the murmurs of Nick's sisters, and Rebecca could be overheard asking, "What's going on, Mom? What are they doing in there?"

Angela shushed her daughter, and led them away from the kitchen. Once the door swung closed, Paige released the breath she'd been holding.

Nick's withdrew his hand from between her legs, but he didn't move away. "I'm sorry."

Her face flamed. Her fingers fumbled with the buttons of her blouse, until he pushed hers away and did it himself. God, she'd behaved shamelessly. She'd let him kiss and caress her in his mother's kitchen. How embarrassing.

"I'll never be able to face your mother again," she muttered in dismay.

Nick dropped his head onto her shoulder. His breathing had yet to return to normal. "I'll talk to her."

"That'll make it worse," she moaned.

"I'll take care of it, don't worry," he reassured her. His hands trailed away, leaving heat in his wake. Paige berated herself over and over again, calling herself ten kinds of fool for getting caught in a heated clinch with

Nick. She scrubbed the dishes furiously, trying to calm down. *Think of something else.* Maybe when she was done, the color in her cheeks would subside and she could face Nick's family once again.

* * * * *

As soon as Nick stepped onto the porch, his siblings snickered. He sighed. His mother was no fool.

Anthony could barely keep the grin off his face. "Don't you think you're a little too old to be getting caught fooling around in the kitchen, Nick?"

Jason raised his arm. "You go, bro!"

Angela swatted Jason's arm. "Stop that. Nicholas, what are you doing to that poor girl?"

He dropped into a cushioned chair. "What do you mean?"

"You say you're just friends?" Angela asked shrewdly.

Faint color bloomed on his cheeks. "We are. Sort of. I don't know. I can't explain it myself either."

Rebecca rolled her eyes. "He's got the hots for her. He could barely keep his eyes off her while we were eating."

"Thanks, squirt," Nick said dryly.

Rebecca grinned. "You're welcome."

Patricia smiled. "I like her."

"Me, too," Nina piped in.

"You're too old for me to be telling you what to do, Nick," his mother said with a sigh. "Paige is a nice girl. Don't play around with her emotions."

He opened his mouth to respond, but his cell phone rang. He took the call. It was his buddy in the crime lab, wanting to see him. He pocketed his phone and stood up. "I gotta go to the station."

He bent and kissed his mother's cheek. "Don't worry so much," he whispered in her ear. With a wave, he headed to the kitchen and got Paige. This had something to do with the murder Paige had witnessed. He'd asked his friend to let him know if anything came up in the examination of evidence collected at the scene. Something interesting must have come up, and he needed to find out what.

*****

"Are you sure?"

The forensic pathologist nodded. "DNA came back with a match, Nick. The mall killer is the same man that killed your sister."

Stunned, Nick spoke slowly, "I need you to be sure, Matt."

Matt Ryder returned Nick's gaze with a steady one of his own. "The DNA we recovered from under Stella Kramer's fingernails matches the DNA we recovered from your sister's apartment."

Nick took a deep breath. His heart pounded. This was the break they'd been waiting for in Cecilia's unsolved murder. "But his MO was different. Cecilia's killer stalked her for weeks before he broke into her apartment."

"We're examining the victim's computer now. In the case of your sister, we found that the killer had sent her anonymous emails a couple of days before he attacked her." Matt paused. "We're going as fast as we can, Nick. We're combing over every inch of the victim's apartment. We're going through her phone messages, her mail." He shrugged. "Maybe something happened to force the killer to change his MO this time. But DNA doesn't lie, Nick."

Lips tightening grimly, Nick nodded. "Paige is in even more danger than we originally thought."

"Until we find out more, her life could very well be at risk." Matt glanced at Paige, who was sitting in the visitor's waiting room. "I'll keep in touch."

Nick shook Matt's hand. "Thanks."

"Don't mention it," Matt said. "Rest assured that we're doing everything we can to get physical evidence in this case, Nick. We're going through the database to cross check evidence from other murders that were possibly committed by the same killer. I hate to say it, but we have a serial killer on our hands."

This was big, bigger than he'd originally thought. If his sister's killer was the same man that committed the mall murder, it was his chance to give his family closure. Getting the guy and throwing his ass in jail for the rest of his life would finally give his sister peace.

* * * * *

Paige waited while Nick talked to a man wearing a white lab coat. Her eyes feasted on him. In his jeans and long-sleeved sweater, Nick looked casual and infinitely sexy. It was her undoing that she couldn't seem to resist him. Her cheeks flamed in embarrassment. Being discovered by his mother with his hand down her pants was mortifying. She still didn't know how she had managed to say her goodbyes to his whole family. Fortunately, Nick hadn't said much in the car on the way over here, sparing her further discomfort.

Paige was quickly figuring out that she had a weakness for rich, coffee-colored eyes and a disarming grin. Nick was sexy as hell, and way too experienced for her. But her body didn't seem to understand that, even though her mind did. In the age-old tradition of women wanting the wrong men, she was in deep. Every time he so much as came within a few feet of her, her body went on high alert. She couldn't explain it. For that matter, science couldn't either. How many studies had she read in medical school about the inexplicable physical attraction that drew males and females together?

She threw him another furtive glance. Nick stood straight and tall, his muscular chest stretching the soft wool of his sweater. The strong muscles of his thighs showed in the jeans he wore. He was a man who commanded a woman's attention and held it.

And he wanted her. That she was sure of.

Plain Paige Harrington. Sure, she was passably attractive if she took the time to fix herself up and put on some makeup. But who had the time to put forth such an effort? Not her. Not with the long, grueling shifts she had to work at the hospital.

So what hope did she have of keeping a man like Nick Santorelli? He'd probably never met a woman like her. She was just a novelty. And novelties were notorious for wearing off quickly.

Nick came up to her and took her elbow. "Let's go."

She observed him while he bundled her in the car, and waited until he pulled out onto the light evening traffic before she spoke. "Is something wrong?"

"No," he replied in a curt voice, frowning at her. He seemed distracted.

"Nick?"

He turned to her.

"Tell me what's wrong."

To her surprise, he pulled over and threw the car into park. His silence was beginning to scare her. Something was very wrong.

"They've discovered some very important evidence about the murder."

Her heart beat a rapid tattoo in her chest. "Is it bad?"

Nick's jaw tightened. "They've recovered DNA from the victim, Stella Kramer. It matches DNA from a previous case."

Cold fingers of fear slithered down her spine. "What do you mean?"

"It means he's killed before. We're dealing with a serial killer here, Paige. More importantly, evidence suggests he's the same man that killed my sister."

Paige covered her mouth with a trembling hand. "Oh, God."

"This changes everything."

A thousand questions flitted through her mind, but Nick's closed expression made her hesitate. It was obvious the discovery that the killer was the same one who murdered his sister was a shock to him.

As he pulled into traffic once again, she reached out and put her hand over his. After a moment, he enfolded her hand in his. No words were necessary. The simple touch expressed their feelings clearer than any words could.

Neither one of them saw the dark-colored van pull out into traffic moments after they did, following them at a safe distance, all the way home.

Chapter Five

The front of the apartment building was dark, illuminated by a single bulb hanging over the front door. Sitting on a low wall across the street, Nick glanced up at the fourth-floor bedroom window of Paige's apartment. It was dark. She'd announced earlier that she was going to turn in. He hadn't said anything, just nodded in agreement. In fact, he hadn't said much since they left the forensics lab. He'd gone downstairs, needing some fresh air. Finding out that the same perp who murdered his sister committed the murder at the mall made this a whole new ball game. A serial killer was on the loose.

Paige was the only one who'd seen the killer's face and lived to tell about it.

He pulled out his cell phone. His father was the first call he made, and he quickly got him up to speed. Nick told him everything he knew, promising to let him know if anything else happened.

"I'll tell your mother," his father said quietly. "Be careful, Son."

"I will, Dad," he answered.

The next call he made was to his brother, Anthony. As the phone was ringing he noticed a young woman entering Paige's building. He recognized her as the woman Paige had pointed out earlier that lived in the apartment next door to her. A man dressed in a long dark coat stopped the door with his hand and slipped in after her. The young woman looked back in surprise. They exchanged a few words then the man trailed after her into the elevator.

Nick stiffened. He didn't like the looks of him. Every instinct on high alert, he jumped off the wall and sprinted across the street. He dialed police dispatch. "This is Detective Nick Santorelli, badge number 5540. I need immediate backup at 15415 8th Street, apartment G. I need backup *now*."

Pocketing his phone, Nick used his key card to activate the door. A quick glance at the elevator confirmed that the old clunker was slowly making its way to the second floor.

He had a bad feeling about this.

Running to the stairs, Nick took the steps two at a time. Pulling open the door to the fourth-floor hallway, he ran to Paige's apartment and locked the door behind him. He pulled his gun from his holster, flicking off the safety.

He went into Paige's bedroom. In the faint moonlight, he could just make out her form on top of the bed. She slept on her side, her hand under her cheek.

He clapped a hand over her mouth.

Her eyes flew open. His hand muffled her scream.

"Shh," he whispered in urgent tones. "Get up. Now."

Paige pushed herself up, rubbing her eyes. "What's going on?"

"We're getting out of here." He motioned for her to be quiet, pulling her along. He barely gave her time to slip on some shoes before he pulled her into the darkened living room.

The doorknob rattled. Somebody was trying to break in.

Paige froze, clutching his hand tightly.

Pushing her behind him, he guided her into the kitchen. "Don't move."

Fear shone in the jade depths of her eyes. "Nick—"

He clasped her arms. "If anything happens, I want you to run like hell out of here. Do you understand me?"

She shook her head. "I'm not going anywhere without you."

"Goddammit, Paige," he whispered fiercely. "Don't argue with me."

Sheer terror was written in her face. "Please. I don't want to leave you."

His jaw ticked. The rattling of the knob broke the silence. They both looked at the door. Nick took a deep breath. Damn it, he needed to get her out of here now.

The fire escape.

He pulled her back to her bedroom, locking the bedroom door. He twisted open the window and made sure the coast was clear. He pushed her out to the fire escape just as the front door crashed open.

Heart pounding, he followed Paige down the creaking metal stairs.

Paige lost her footing, stumbling down the steps.

Nick pulled her up. "Go!"

With a choked whimper, Paige ran down the stairs, Nick close at her heels. Above them, the glass window burst open and crashed into a thousand tiny pieces. Sharp shards of glass rained over their heads.

Nick fired a shot. The loud blast echoed into the night. A male voice cursed above. Paige jumped the remaining steps down to the ground. Nick grabbed her wrist and pulled her to his car. Pushing her unceremoniously inside, he ran to the other side and started the car. They pulled away with squealing tires, driving away into the darkness of the night.

Paige trembled violently.

Nick didn't slow down. He needed to get her to safety first. How the hell had that happened? How had he missed it? Had they been followed from the police station? His thoughts raced. He had almost failed her. Goddammit, why hadn't she listened when he'd told her to go without him? He could have gone back and faced the bastard.

"Next time I tell you to do something, you better goddamn follow the order," he said in cold fury. "If I tell you to go, you *go*. Without question, do you understand me, Paige?"

"I'm sorry—"

"You're *sorry*? That's all you can say? Your safety is my first concern. Don't disobey me again."

Tears glistened in her eyes, but she snapped back, "I said I was sorry."

Nick noted she was trembling violently. Blood was running down her right arm. He cursed. "Why the hell didn't you tell me you were hurt?" he barked. He pulled off the road and threw the car into park. "Let me see that."

She turned away. "It's nothing."

He gritted his teeth. "Let me be the judge of that."

"I'm a doctor. Believe me when I tell you it's nothing," she bit out.

Seeing her shaking and injured, all his anger drained instantly away. Her teeth were chattering. Shock was probably setting in. All things considered, she was remarkably composed. In her pajamas, her hair tousled and her face pale, she sat still and cradled her arm against her side.

Without a word, he pulled her into his arms. Paige sat stiffly at first, before gradually relaxing and leaning into him. He didn't let her go until her shaking subsided. "Let me see where you're hurt."

She didn't protest when he gently took her arm. The gash wasn't deep, but it was still bleeding.

"We need to get that cleaned up," he declared before shaking his head. "Why am I telling you this? You're a doctor. You know what to do." His hand came up and rubbed her cheek. "Are you okay?"

"I'm all right." She fell silent before she raised her eyes to his. "What if he'd gotten to me? What would you have done?" Fear lingered in her gaze.

He pushed her hair away from her face. "I would have done everything I could to save you, do you hear me?" It was important to him that she believed he would never let anything happen to her. "I'll tell you this, if ever he gets to you first, I will not hesitate to kill him. I won't let him hurt you, do you understand?" he asked fiercely.

"And if he takes me hostage? What then?" Paige felt compelled to ask.

He didn't hesitate. "All I need is a fraction of a second for him to get distracted and I'll shoot." He understood the fear that she felt.

She nodded, looking utterly vulnerable. Nick bent and brushed her lips with his. Her lips parted, her face tilted toward his. Unable to help himself, his hand curved under her nape and he swooped in. He kissed her, long and deep. He never would have forgiven himself if anything happened to her tonight.

"I have to take you somewhere safe," he said softly. "But first, I have to take care of some things." He pulled out his cell phone and punched in some numbers. "Anthony, it's me. I need you to meet me at the coffee shop on First and Broadway. Bring the duffel bag I left in your garage. And get some clothes from Rebecca for Paige to use. Will you swing by my house and pick up the Jeep? I need another car. This one's been made." He paused. "Yeah, the bastard broke into her apartment tonight. I need to get her somewhere safe."

* * * * *

Paige looked at her reflection in the mirror. The shirt was too tight. Without the benefit of a bra, her ample breasts pushed against the soft cotton of the shirt. Her face warmed. Rebecca was a size smaller. The jeans fit her like a glove, the hip-hugger style hanging low on her. She tried to pull the shirt down to cover the patch of skin revealed by the low-slung jeans, but it didn't work. Pulling down the shirt only emphasized her breasts more. Why hadn't Anthony brought her a jacket or something to cover up?

Squaring her shoulders, Paige walked out of the restroom. As she approached the table, she observed Nick's eyes narrow.

"What the hell are you wearing?"

With a self-conscious blush, Paige glared right back. "I'm wearing what your brother brought."

His dark eyes drifted down to her chest.

To her mortification, her nipples pebbled under his gaze. Heat curled in her stomach.

"Did he forget to bring you a bra, too?" he muttered.

Paige resisted the impulse to cover her chest with her arms. "I guess he didn't think it was a necessity."

Nick looked behind her. "Sit down," he bit out.

Lips tightening in annoyance, Paige slid inside the booth. "Stop glaring at me."

The muscle in his jaw ticked. "Eat."

Why the hell was he so mad at her? "I'm not hungry."

"We have a long drive ahead of us. I suggest you eat something."

Paige lifted her chin. "I can't force myself to eat, Nick."

He threw down some bills on the table. "Fine. Let's go." Sliding out of the booth, he clamped a hand on her uninjured arm and pulled her behind him.

As soon as they were outside, Paige shook off his arm. "Why are you so mad at me? What did I do now?"

Nick whirled around. "Didn't you see every man in that coffee shop staring at you?"

Her anger flared to match his. "I didn't invite their attention. May I remind you that the last thing I want is to draw attention to myself?"

"It's the fucking clothes you're wearing," he bit out.

Her eyes widened in disbelief. "And that's my fault? Your brother brought me these clothes. Why don't you take me back home so I can get my own clothes?"

"Your building is now a crime scene," he growled. "A young woman was found dead in the elevator."

Paige gasped. "Oh my God."

He pulled her along and opened the door to the Jeep. "Get in."

Numbly, she got in. "Who was it?"

He didn't even glance at her as he started the car. "Your neighbor. The killer followed her into the building and killed her in the elevator."

Tears came to her eyes. "But why?"

His eyes turned hard. "Because she's another witness, Paige. Now do you realize the enormity of the situation you're in? This man wants to kill you, and he'll stop at *nothing* to get to you."

Chapter Six

Paige slumped against the leather seat. Her neighbor had been a friendly young woman who was studying at the university. Poor Diana. Her family was going to be devastated. Over and over, she replayed the scene in her head. The stark terror she had felt was a reminder of how lucky she was Nick was there to protect her.

The scenery passed in a blur. She settled deeper into the seat, unable to relax. The Jeep was roomier and more comfortable than the old car. Anthony had taken the sedan Nick had been using, and promised to drop it off at the police station.

"Where are we going?" she asked.

"I'm taking you somewhere safe. Try to get some sleep. We'll be there in about an hour."

"Nick, I need to call my father."

"I've called Captain Ridgeway. He's going to call your father and inform him of the latest development," he replied. "I'd rather not tell anybody where we're going, Paige. It's just a precaution."

"I can't just up and leave, Nick. What about my job? The hospital needs me."

"They're going to have to do without you for a few days. Ridgeway said he'll take care of your boss at the hospital."

"I don't like this."

"You don't have to like it," he retorted. "My job is to keep you alive and that's what I'm going to do." His fingers tightened on the steering wheel. "They're combing the whole building for fingerprints. With any luck, we won't have to be gone for more than a few days."

"Why do we have to go so far?" But as soon as she said the words, she knew the answer.

His eyes flashed in irritation. "How do you think he knew where you lived? He followed us home, Paige, most likely from the station. If you take a chance and stay close to home, he'll find you again."

That shut her up. There was a killer out to get her. She'd do well to remember that and not get hot and bothered by the heated looks Nick kept giving her. So why wouldn't he stop looking at her? She squirmed in her seat, feeling heated moisture in her pussy. *Here I go again.* One look from him and she was ready to burst into flames.

Her breath hissed from between her lips. Crossing her arms in front of her chest, she looked out the window into the darkness of the night. There were a number of studies that suggested sexual arousal increased after an adrenaline rush. Maybe that's what was happening here. She frowned. Taking several relaxing breaths, she averted her face and concentrated on calming down. Don't look at him. Just don't look at him.

Nick was pretty sure he'd left his tongue somewhere on the floor of the coffee shop. Dressed in his sister's clothes, which looked to be about a size too small, Paige was a knockout. The shirt, which fit her like a glove, molded her generous breasts faithfully. He wasn't the only one who'd noticed. A hot flare of irritation had hit him when the other men in the coffee shop had eyed her with interest. He'd swept her out of there as soon as he could.

The unfamiliar feeling of jealousy hit him like a ton of bricks.

What the hell was the matter with him? So what if other men were looking at her? So what if he spied more than one man leering at her tight ass? It had never bothered him before to have other men admire the woman he was with. Why was Paige different? He didn't know. All he knew was that it had been the final straw when the man seated in the booth across from theirs openly ogled her breasts.

He had been less then gentle when he'd pulled her to the car. It wasn't her fault that men were staring at her. The clothes weren't even hers. What was unprecedented was the possessiveness that consumed him. His fingers clenched on the steering wheel. He didn't want to analyze why he felt that way.

He glanced at her. She was looking out the window, stiff and unmoving. *Great.* Now she was pissed at him, too. Her crossed arms pushed her breasts up, emphasizing the fullness of their shape.

Maybe it was better. The sight of her unfettered breasts had aroused him quickly and painfully. He grimaced. It was damned uncomfortable to have his cock try to push its way out of his pants. If she wasn't talking to him, maybe his cock would stand down and his eyes would finally stray from her chest. And maybe he'd stop feeling the insistent fingers of arousal stoking the fire in his blood.

His cock hardened even more.

With a rueful shake of his head, Nick shifted in his seat. His body was behaving like a hormone-driven sixteen-year-old looking forward to his first time. He rolled down the window of the Jeep. The crisp, invigorating night air hit his face. But it did nothing to cool him off.

In the dim interior of the vehicle, he could just make out her profile. His arm was inches away from her leg. All he had to do was reach out and he'd be able to touch her. He glanced at the luscious stretch of leg covered by tight denim. Damn. The Doc looked entirely too sexy in those jeans. His fingers flexed on the steering wheel. *Get your mind off her and think of something else.*

With the traffic minimal, the drive to the beach cottage took just under an hour. It was after midnight when he pulled up in front of the dark and secluded cabin. He switched the headlights off and waited, making sure they weren't followed. The street was dark and deserted. No sign of another car.

He got out. The smell of the salty sea air was refreshing. The waves crashed on the beach a short distance away. Anthony had bought the cabin some years ago as a weekend getaway. Other than family, nobody knew about it. Paige should be safe here for a few days while his colleagues at the police department hunted down leads.

He made a quick trip around the cottage, checking out the perimeter. It was located on a quiet street, just two blocks from the beach. A single bulb illuminated the porch. Walking back to the Jeep, he pulled open the door and gently shook Paige awake.

"Paige, we're here."

Sleep-darkened jade eyes slowly focused on him. "We're here, where?"

"Anthony's cabin. We're about a half-hour away from San Diego," he explained. He opened the trunk and pulled out his duffel bag and a small overnight bag packed with some essentials that Anthony had brought for her. He unlocked the front door and ushered her in, flipping on the lights. The cabin was small, with one bedroom, a living room-dining room combo and a functional kitchen. Walking directly to the bedroom, Nick dropped the bags on the floor.

Paige stopped at the sight of the king-sized bed. "Where do I sleep?"

With a tilt of his head, Nick indicated the lone bed. "Are you wondering where I'm sleeping?"

She flushed at his mocking tone. "Yes."

"It's a small cabin, Paige. Used for weekends and quick getaways. There isn't another bed in the whole place." When she didn't respond, he continued, "Look. I'm not sleeping on that couch, if you can even call it that. It's small and cramped, and too short for me. It's a big bed. We can probably each stay on our side with plenty of space to spare." He threw her a challenging stare. "Will that be a problem for you?"

Her gaze slid to the couch. "I'll take that, then."

He shrugged, disappointed. "Suit yourself."

"I will."

Nick fought back a grin. "Okay then."

"Fine," she snapped. "I'd like to freshen up."

He pointed to a door at the rear of the bedroom. "Right through there."

She turned to go, and then halted. "I, uh, need a shirt to sleep in. Do you have an extra one I can use?" At his frown, she explained, "My pajamas were stained with blood from the cut on my arm. I had to throw them away."

Nick rifled through his duffel bag and pulled out a shirt. "Here."

With murmured thanks, she headed to the bathroom. She was stubborn as hell, but she'd learn. The wicker couch was the size of a loveseat. He would have had to sleep curled up in a ball to fit his frame in there. Nick glanced at the bed. There was plenty of room for both of them. But if she wanted to sleep in discomfort on a small couch, then it was up to her. He certainly didn't.

He strode to the kitchen and opened the refrigerator and cupboards. He made a note to swing by the grocery store tomorrow to get some supplies. He picked up the phone. It was working. He walked around the small cottage, checking doors and windows. He stayed out there until he heard the shower turn off. He gave her a few minutes before he went directly to the bathroom.

The chilly shower helped cool his heated body somewhat, but his stiff cock had a mind of its own. Damn thing never did listen to him. Too bad she'd decided to take the couch. He'd actually looked forward to sharing a bed with her.

She'd rather sleep on the couch, would she? Well, she'd find out soon enough that it was uncomfortable as hell. He wouldn't be the only one suffering tonight. A smug grin formed on his lips. Doctor Paige Harrington was going to be mighty sorry when she woke up.

Paige turned this way and that on the small wicker couch. Try as she might, she just couldn't find a comfortable position. As it was, her legs were bent, pretzel-like, as she tried to squeeze herself in the short space. She gave the wide open bedroom door a murderous glance. *He's probably asleep already. Chivalry is dead, that's for sure.* After a few futile minutes, she grabbed the pillow and blanket and tossed them on the floor.

The floor was no better. Her back was going to kill her tomorrow. What the hell, she wouldn't have gotten any sleep next to him anyway. She punched the pillow and turned on her side. Her elbow came into contact with the thick, squat leg of the coffee table. A sharp shaft of pain hit her. "Ow!"

Nick came out from the bedroom and stood over her, his arms crossed. "What the hell is going on?"

Paige rubbed her elbow. "Nothing. Go back to sleep."

He had the nerve to grin. "Who can sleep with the racket you're making?"

She glared at him, her eyes sliding from his chest to his washboard stomach. "Racket?" she repeated with disdain.

He chuckled. "Come on, Doc. Don't let your pride get in the way of a good night's sleep. That bed is plenty big enough for both us."

"No thanks. I'm perfectly fine here," she replied in a prim voice. *Don't look at his toned chest and ripped muscles and his oh-so touchable skin. Think of a myocardial contusion. The bruising on the chest wall…* She shrieked as he unceremoniously picked her up from the floor.

"What do you think you're doing?" she hissed, outraged.

"One of us has got to show some common sense," he said in a dry voice. "It's obvious it's me." Like a sack of potatoes, he dropped her on the bed.

Paige's outrage was replaced by a gasp as the shirt rode up her thighs. *Oh no, he'd see—*

Nick froze.

Dark red color crept up her cheeks. The shirt ended up on her stomach, baring her body for him to see.

"Paige." His voice pulsed with desire. His eyes blazed like molten lava as he stared at her. "Jesus. You're not wearing anything under that shirt?"

Her response was instantaneous. Seeing the naked desire shining in his eyes, Paige was helpless to stop her body's reaction. Her nipples tightened into two aching points. Heat swirled in her belly, starting a chain reaction until she was caught, helpless and aching, in the face of a firestorm. Paige didn't move, couldn't move. She let him look his fill.

"Apparently, your brother didn't think underwear was a necessity either," she replied, her voice husky, a little defiant.

He uttered a sound somewhere between a snort and a grunt. "He's a man. What do you expect?"

Paige licked her lips. "I had to wash the pair I was wearing." Her fingers moved to the hem of the shirt.

"Don't."

That one word, throbbing with lust, stopped her.

"Just let me look at you." His tortured voice had her breath hitching in the back of her throat. He sounded pained. Her gaze dropped to his front. The impressive length of his cock was straining the soft cotton of his boxers. She moistened her suddenly dry lips.

"Stop that," he growled.

Her eyes flew to his. "Why?"

"You're not helping here, Paige."

He was affected by the sight of her body, and he couldn't hide it. She felt the purely feminine power of being able to arouse Nick Santorelli. In a movement as old as Eve herself, she moved her hips sensuously and parted her thighs.

Nick choked. He put a knee on the bed. "This is insanity. We shouldn't be doing this. Tell me to stop right here, right now, Paige."

Paige didn't stop to think. The heat in his eyes gave her the courage to pull the shirt over her head. He wanted her and she gloried in the knowledge. He made her feel beautiful. "Do you want to stop, Nick?"

Her words issued a challenge, but her voice issued an invitation. She wanted him to admit he wanted her and act upon it.

Before she drew her next breath, he was on top of her. He grasped her wrists and held them over her head. "Once we cross this line, there's no going back."

Her senses reeled. Her skin was hot wherever they touched. Every breath she took pushed her closer to him. "What are you saying?"

His dark, velvety eyes slid down to her moist lips. "No barriers, Paige. No inhibition. You give me everything I ask for. No questions asked. No hesitation."

Was she ready for this? Could she do this?

He breathed harshly. "I need a woman who will give me everything she has to give. That's what I want, what I need. You have to be sure you're willing to do that."

Yes. Paige had never been surer of anything. She wanted to be everything he wanted and needed. She wanted to be with him. "That's what I want, too." Her lips parted in a sultry smile. "I want to put your cock in my mouth and suck it. I want to swallow. I want to try different positions, Nick. I want to do them all with you."

That was all it took to push him over the edge. Nick pounced on her, his tongue plunging deep inside her mouth. He took her breath and made it his own. His big body curved over her, enclosing her in a fiery cocoon. One muscular leg pushed between her thighs, his soft body hair causing a pleasant abrasion against her skin.

"Lesson number one. Check your inhibitions at the door. No shyness. No modesty." He brushed her lips with his, once, twice. "I want you naked all the time."

Boldly licking the corners of his lips, she murmured, "I'm an eager student." Taking him by surprise, she slid her tongue between his lips.

"No turning back now." He slid down the length of her neck, pausing to suck the skin right where her pulse beat madly at the base of her throat.

Paige arched and strained against his hold. "Don't I get to touch you, too?"

"Later," he muttered. He trailed his hand down her front, drawing circles around her breast. Her nipple tightened in anticipation. He went around and around in ever smaller circles, but stopped short of touching the tip. Paige stifled a moan.

"Have I told you that your breasts are incredible?" he whispered. "They're full and generous, just the right size for my hand." He swiped a distended tip, his lips curving when she moaned. "Tell me what you're feeling."

Paige's eyes flew open. He wanted to talk? *Now*?

"Paige?" Nick prompted.

It was hard to concentrate with the light touch that was tracing her nipple.

"Talk to me, Paige," he murmured, tickling her with his breath.

She arched her back, trying to push more of her flesh into his elusive hand. "I-I don't think I can."

Nick skimmed the tops of her breasts. "Tell me what you want me to do."

"I want you to put my breast inside your mouth."

Satisfaction glinted in his eyes. "What else?"

Inhaling deeply, she bravely went on. "Suck me deep."

As a reward, he pulled the tight tip deep and sucked hard.

Paige came off the bed, her whimper breaking the silence of the room. Sharp pleasure shot straight through every nerve ending in her body. The strong, rhythmic suction of his lips drove her insane.

"Nick," she gasped.

He released her, and her arms fell limply on the bed. He cupped the tempting mounds in each hand, kneading and squeezing. She tossed her head back and forth. He scraped her gently with his teeth then soothed her with a swipe of his tongue.

Nick put her hand on her breast. "I want you to touch yourself," he instructed in a low, seductive voice. Noting her hesitation, he drew back. "You've never touched yourself? Never made yourself come?"

Though she was embarrassed at her lack of experience, she didn't look away. "I've never done that."

Nick pulled her up off the bed and in front of the mirrored closet door. "Look at yourself, Paige. You're a beautiful, sexy woman."

Paige swallowed, looking instead at him.

"Don't look at me, sweetheart." He shifted to stand behind her. "There's nothing wrong with exploring yourself and learning what gives you pleasure." He trailed his fingers up to the swells of her breasts. "The human body is made to give and receive pleasure. There's no shame in it."

He teased the peak of her breast into pouting tightness. "Feel that?" he asked. "When I take your nipple between my fingers like this—" he took the distended tip between thumb and forefinger "—and I pinch it like this—" he squeezed just enough to send sparks of fire shooting through her body "—your body burns, warm and waiting for the next rush of pleasure."

She inhaled deeply.

He brought her hands up to her breasts, covering them with his. Under his guidance, her palms rotated over the hard tips. "I want you with me every step of the way. I want you to be a willing participant."

Paige shuddered.

Under his gentle but insistent control, her hand glided down over the slight swell of her stomach to the soft curls that guarded her pussy. "Yes." His voice was no more than a breath inside her ear. "Slide your fingers inside your pussy. Feel the wetness between your legs."

She whimpered as she obeyed. Her own juices coated her fingers, warm and fluid.

"Open your legs wider, baby."

She widened her stance. He plunged their fingers deep into her slick core. "It feels good, doesn't it, Paige? Imagine how it feels when I'm inside you."

The slow thrusting motion drove her crazy. The rough, callused pad of his thumb brushed again and again against her clit. A violent tremor rocked her. She gasped.

"Stay right there." Nick walked out and came right back in, pulling a chair in his wake. He quickly shucked his shorts before he sat down and pulled Paige on top of him, positioning her legs on the outside of his. She was splayed wide in front of the mirror, her cleft open and visible.

"Don't look away," he instructed roughly.

Her breath rushed between her lips. Even if she'd wanted to, she couldn't look away. The picture they made was erotic and utterly sexual. Pleasure bolted up her spine. She could feel his cock snuggle disturbingly between the cheeks of her ass. Rubbing against the stiff length, she felt a twinge of nervousness. He felt huge.

How on earth would he fit?

Nick chuckled, a strained, strangled sound. "Don't worry, I'll fit."

She licked her lips, squirming against him. In the next second, all sane thought flew from her mind. Nick pulled her glistening labia apart, exposing her to both their gazes. Her flesh was pink and slick with moisture. Her clit, stiff and pulsing, stood out among the soft, wet folds.

"You're so fucking beautiful," he rasped against her ear.

Paige bit back a moan. She could hardly recognize the wanton creature that stared back at her. There was no sign on the old insecure, unconfident Paige. The one sitting on top of Nick was flushed with arousal, her skin damp with perspiration. Excitement blazed in her eyes, and her lips trembled with need.

"Delicious," he muttered. He made a passing swipe at her clit.

Paige jerked in his arms.

"So responsive. I can't wait until I push my dick up in your pussy, Paige. I can't wait until I feel you all around me, hot and tight, begging me to fuck you deeper, harder."

Paige moaned.

He guided her hand to her throbbing clit. "Touch yourself, baby. Yeah, just like that."

She rubbed around and around, spreading the ever-gathering moisture around the slick folds of her pussy. In a daze, she stared at the mirror, mesmerized by the sight. Even when he let go, she didn't stop. It felt good. Too good…

Nick blazed a trail of fire up to the aching mounds of her breasts. He pushed and pulled, squeezed and tugged at her nipples. Her whole universe centered on the sensations swirling around her. Nothing else in the world existed except the fingers that were driving her crazy.

"Take yourself over the edge, baby. Come for me," he growled against her skin.

Her hips writhed, pushing against her finger. "Nick, Nick," she chanted with mindless abandon.

"I'm right here, Paige. Just let go."

At his huskily spoken words, pleasure exploded in a kaleidoscope of colors behind her fluttering eyelids. She jerked violently in his arms. Huge waves of ecstasy slammed into her, robbing her of breath. Paige ground her hips onto his, sobbing her pleasure. It was unbearable. She never wanted it to end.

She didn't know how much time had passed. Her mind still spun hazily from the eye-opening experience she just had. Slowly, the soothing words Nick murmured penetrated her consciousness. The tremors that shook her eased gradually as she slumped back against him.

He rained soft kisses on her cheek. "Thank you for letting me see that. That was amazing. You were so open, so passionate." Nick touched his lips to her, giving her a slow, deep kiss.

The fires that were temporarily banked flared to life again, sending heat swirling in the pit of her stomach. The kiss turned hard, as hard as the knot of pleasure tightening in her belly. He tore his lips from hers, only to lift her off his lap and put his cock against her pussy. Drawn to their reflection in the mirror, Paige stared at the mushroom-shaped head nestled between soft, slick folds. A knot rose in her throat. He was thick and wide, and oh-so big.

He rubbed his cock up and down against her slit. A quiver worked its way through her skin. The soft tissues of her labia yielded to his touch, lovingly clinging to his stiff cock. Again and again, he rubbed. Up and down. Over and around. Paige moaned in rising excitement. She wanted more.

Grasping his cock, Nick slipped the broad head inside her slit. A whimper escaped her lips. He was so hot, so thick. Her heart hammered against her ribs at his slow progress. She wanted all of him—now.

"Please," she panted.

He withdrew. "Please what?"

She was nearly insane and murmured incoherently.

"Tell me what you want." He slid his cock up and down her pussy, spreading the warm evidence of her arousal. "No shyness, remember? You can tell me anything you want."

Her thoughts spun from the blood pounding in her brain. No shyness. No inhibitions. Through the haze of arousal, she realized what he wanted from her. The harsh uneven rhythm of her breathing sounded loud in the silence of the room. She met his gaze bravely in the mirror. "I want you to fuck me."

His arms tightened around her in response. His breath felt hot against her ear.

"I need you inside me, Nick," she entreated, emboldened by the heat in his eyes. Was that husky, needy voice really hers? "I need to feel all of you inside me."

Nick grasped her hips and lifted her up. She instinctively braced her feet on the seat. What she saw took what little breath she had left. His cock stood straight up, a thick, purple-headed shaft of steel poised at the entrance to her pussy.

Nick lowered her inch by painful inch. She gasped. He slipped in, pushing through the soft, yielding tissues. He was huge. Paige whimpered as she melted against him. He wasn't even in halfway.

"You okay?" he asked through gritted teeth.

She nodded, caught in the grip of a blinding lust, unable to speak.

He pushed up, at the same time pulling her down. She inhaled sharply as he filled her in one stroke, reaching all the way to her womb. A soft moan of bliss escaped her lips. "It feels so…" she trailed off, unable to find the words to describe what she was feeling.

Nick grunted, shifting to adjust her on top of him. Paige trembled, every movement reminding her of the cock filling her. "Brace your hands here," he instructed, indicating the armrests. His breath was coming hard and fast, just like hers. "Now move up and down, baby. You set the pace."

So she moved, gingerly at first. The initial discomfort she felt was gone. Instead, she derived nothing but pleasure with every down stroke of her hips. She bit her lip. His cock penetrated the innermost folds of her pussy, filling every inch. Planting her feet firmly outside his knees, she gained momentum. Going faster, sinking deeper, taking his whole stiff length in her. In. Out. She was desperate for more.

"You feel so good," he whispered in a pleasure-roughened voice. He toyed with her breasts, tugging at her distended nipples. He dragged hot fingertips over her belly down to her pussy. He pulled open the slick lips, exposing her stiff clit.

The sight of his cock buried so deep in her was something she'd never forget.

"Beautiful." He flicked at her clit. Her strangled gasp rushed from her throat. "You like that?" Again and again, he tortured her with alternating light and forceful touches that drove her crazy. "Feel how your clit is pushing against my finger, asking for more."

Paige had lost the ability to speak. The sensations coursing through her were fast, escalating out of control. Little mewling noises came from the back of her throat, increasing in intensity with every slap of her hips against his. Her hands clenched on the armrests, holding on tight. Her skin was damp with perspiration. Her breasts jiggled as she bounced on his lap.

Nick tipped her chin toward him. His mouth covered hers hungrily. Higher and higher she climbed, spiraling toward ecstasy. Tingles raced up and down her body, signaling the arrival of another orgasm.

He gripped her hips and fucked her in a series of mind-blowing, violent thrusts. She tore her lips from his, panting heavily. Nick was without mercy now, intent on pushing them over the edge. *God, she was almost there…*

With a soft scream, Paige shattered.

Her eyes drifted shut as pleasure exploded inside her. Trembling from the force that hit her, she ground her hips against his. Rapture rolled through her in huge waves. She'd lost all sense of time and space. The shudders went on and on, an explosion of pent-up desire.

"Jesus," she heard him mutter somewhere behind her. His arms came around her, anchoring her securely to him. He gave one mighty push and came, filling her pussy with his seed. The muscles of her pussy clung to his cock. Afterwards, she slumped against him, weak and boneless. Utterly spent.

His heartbeat thundered against her back, a sound that somehow soothed her. She stirred as Nick dropped a tender kiss on her shoulder.

"You just passed lesson number one with flying colors."

Chapter Seven

Nick gazed at Paige. She was sleeping peacefully, her hand under one side of her face. Impossibly long, sooty lashes rested on her flushed cheeks, and her lips were slightly parted. She looked young and innocent.

Who would have guessed that inside that innocent was a sexy, passionate woman? Memories of their heated coupling raced through his mind. His cock stirred. She had matched him step for step and kept up with every stroke. She'd displayed an amazing, untapped capacity for passion. The prim and proper doctor who hid her looks under loose clothing and no makeup was one hot-blooded woman.

With his fingertips, he traced the soft arch of her back. Her skin was so supple and infinitely touchable. He followed the dip of her waist before stopping at the full curve of her hips. They were generous, meant to cradle a man. Paige Harrington was a very desirable woman. It was only the circumstances by which she grew up that made her unsure of her appeal. He grinned wryly. That was good for him. He liked assuming the role of her teacher. He loved the thought of showing her the world of pleasure they could explore together.

His gaze drifted up to her breasts. The hazy morning light highlighted her ivory skin. The soft mounds were crowned with large, round pale nipples. He shook his head as his cock snapped to full attention. He'd never thought he was a breast man, but hers were just about perfect in his eyes. He cupped them, marveling at how they were just right for his hands. He tugged gently at the nipples, elongating them before bending low to lave one with his tongue. Delicious. He could feast on her for hours. He toyed with the stiff tip, tonguing it over and over.

Paige stirred. Not yet awake, her body warm and relaxed from sleep, she arched into his mouth. Accepting the offering, he opened wide and pulled as much of her flesh into his mouth as he could.

"Hmmm," she murmured, her voice drowsy.

"Good morning," he mumbled, with the nipple in his mouth. He shifted to her other breast and gave it the same thorough attention. He raked the tip gently with his teeth, gratified to feel her shiver.

Her soft "oh" was full of helpless pleasure.

He pushed her onto her back and lay over her. "I'm crazy about your nipples," he declared between little bites and kisses. "They're perfectly round, just the right size for me." He felt her tremble and loved how responsive and sensitive her breasts were.

"Nick," she moaned.

He took one tip between his teeth and bit down gently. It was soft and swollen from his touch—he loved it. He knew she must be tender and a little sore, but he couldn't stop himself. He bit the underside of her breast, earning a loud moan from her. When he looked up, she had pushed herself up on her elbows and was watching him feast on her.

He pinned her with a hot gaze before pulling a nipple deep into his mouth. Her little whimper sailed over his heated senses. He gripped her hips and shifted her under him, positioning his cock over her pussy. Her thighs fell open, making room for him.

"Nick, I can't— " she gasped.

Nick pulled on her just a little bit harder. Beneath him, she was writhing like a wild thing. He grasped her arms and stretched them out to her sides. "Don't move."

Her hair flailed wildly on the pillow as she shook her head. "I d-don't think I can hold still."

He levered himself over her, breaking off all contact. "Do it, Paige." His lips curved in satisfaction when she kept her arms where they were. "Good."

Using both hands, he kneaded her breasts, alternating between firm squeezes and light strokes. "You're so fucking sexy. Does it feel good when I do this?"

Her face was flushed with heat as she nodded. He resumed his caresses, mixing just the right amount of pleasure and pain. Her breathing grew heavier, deeper. He suckled her deep in his mouth, flicking her with the tip of his tongue.

"Ohhhh."

"I want you to come just by me sucking your nipples," he growled.

His words triggered a wild response. She bucked in his arms, her hands clenching on the mussed sheets. With a soft scream, she came. He absorbed the huge tremor that rocked her body and held her tight through the turmoil. When she calmed down, he raked her nipple softly, bringing a fresh round of delicious quivers through her once again.

"I can't believe you did that."

Nick grinned, unrepentant. "I can. I'm crazy about your breasts."

She buried her face in his neck. "They're too big."

He chuckled, a warm sound of pure male amusement. "You say that like it's a bad thing."

"You have an unhealthy obsession with my breasts. A shrink would have a field day with you," she mumbled against his skin.

He captured her lips in a slow, sexy kiss. "Don't ever wear a bra when it's just you and me."

Her breath hitched audibly. "Why?"

"Because I like knowing I can touch you anytime. That I can stick my hand under your shirt and feel you." His voice deepened. "But then I'd also like seeing you wearing one of those tight little bras that barely cover these." His hand swept over her nipples. "Maybe I'll make you wear that and I'll just sit and stare at you."

She made a sound suspiciously like a snort. "You're crazy."

"Although I won't object if you wear a tight shirt, you know," he went on. "The shirt you had on yesterday damn near drove me crazy. These—" he nuzzled the dewy mounds "—were pushing against the shirt, as if begging to be let out. Every man in the coffee shop must have gotten a hard-on the minute you walked in. I know I did."

When she scoffed at that statement, his eyebrow rose. "Sweetheart, let me tell you something. I never thought I'd obsess about breasts. But I'm crazy about these."

She flushed. "Stop it."

Running his hand over her luscious ass, he gave one cheek a firm tap. "Let's go have some breakfast. I want to go to the local mall and get you some clothes to wear." He got up and stood next to the bed. He looked down to find her gaze glued to his erect cock.

He grinned. "Want to join me in the shower?"

Paige blinked. "No, thank you."

Nick grasped his cock and ran his hand up and down the turgid length. "Sure?" Watching the red flush sweep over her cheeks, he could tell she was oh-so tempted. "We could play a little."

She bit her lip and pulled the sheet over her. When she spoke, the sound was no more than a croak. "You go ahead."

He decided to let it drop. "If you change your mind…" he trailed off, heading for the bathroom. A grin fought its way to the surface. If it was the last thing he did, he would make sure Doctor Prim and Proper was left with no inhibitions at all. He was looking forward to it.

* * * * *

The mall was new, sprawling and almost deserted this time of day. Bright sunshine shone through the huge skylight-filled ceilings and the smell of salty air filtered in from the outside. A few shoppers wandered here and there, browsing through shop windows. Nick guided her to a well-known clothing store.

"Pick out what you need," he instructed. When she hesitated, he continued, "I'll take care of it, Paige."

She didn't budge. "I'll pay you when we get back."

His broad shoulders moved in a careless shrug. "Whatever. Now go."

There was no use arguing with him. Paige circled the store, picking out jeans, a couple of shirts, and a sweater. She went up to Nick. "All done."

He eyed the clothes she held in one arm. "Already?"

She shrugged. "I only needed a pair of jeans, and a couple of other things."

Without saying anything, he plucked the clothes from her and inspected them one by one. "These won't do," he declared peremptorily, dropping the offending items on the nearest table. He pulled her along. "Let's go."

The clerk and a customer were giving them curious looks. "What are you doing?" she hissed.

Nick didn't stop until he was in front of the jeans rack. "Your days of wearing loose clothing are over, Paige. You don't need to hide."

Pulling her hand from his, she glared at him. "I'm not hiding. I prefer to wear comfortable clothes."

"You can be comfortable but sexy," he countered in a cool tone. When she stubbornly refused to budge, he went on, "I thought we agreed to leave the old Paige behind."

"I believe I was agreeing to a change of attitude," she argued in a low voice, feeling her face hot with embarrassment. A furtive glance revealed that they were becoming a spectacle.

Nick bent and nuzzled her ear. "Clothes can be comfortable yet sexy, Paige." The light, almost absent, touch of his fingers across her middle made her catch her breath. "Low-slung, hip-hugging jeans are especially tempting. I imagine seeing a flash of delectable skin left bare, soft and silky. It would make me want to touch."

Without even being aware of it, Paige had shifted closer to him. His voice was mesmerizing, his words alluring. The familiar spell he knew how to weave around her worked its magic.

"I'd love to see you in jeans that mold the plump curves of your ass and hug the shape of your legs."

Heat seeped from his skin to hers, warming her instantly. His voice lowered to a sinful whisper, "Pair that with a shirt that skims your belly, which molds your breasts to perfection. That would drive me crazy." He pulled her closer. She felt the awesome length of his erection under the thick material of his jeans. "Don't you want to drive me crazy, Paige?"

Was that a trick question? Her mind was already hazy with familiar arousal. Her resistance weakened in the face of his sensuous persuasion. "Yes."

He captured her lips in an erotic kiss, right in the middle of the store, uncaring of who saw them. It was a slow tangling of tongues that left her senses reeling. She was dazed when it ended, so affected that she wasn't even aware of him picking out some things here and there before pulling her to the register. The heavily made-up teenager shot them a knowing grin before ringing up the purchases.

Her cheeks flamed. Shameless, that's what she was. He'd turned her into a shameless woman. Nick's arm anchored her to his side as they walked out of the store. His touch was possessive, reminding her of the desire simmering just under the surface.

Her lips still tingled from his toe-curling kiss. She couldn't resist running her tongue over them, savoring his taste. Her breasts felt heavy and sensitive as she walked beside him. It was hard to resist the urge to squeeze them for some relief. The moisture drenching her underwear was making it difficult to walk. It didn't help that his hand was like a hot brand on her skin. She felt surrounded, overpowered by the sheer sexual spell he was weaving around her.

It seemed surreal that this big, gorgeous man walking next to her made love to her last night. *Fucked me last night,* she corrected herself. He taught her to enjoy her body, to relish the pleasure it gave her. Well, she'd certainly done that. All the while, watching every single sensual thing he did to drive her out of her mind. It would forever be etched in her mind. The image of an uninhibited woman lost in the throes of pleasure, a woman out of control. If somebody had told her a couple of weeks ago that she was going to be having wild, mind-blowing sex with a handsome detective, she would have laughed.

Nick pulled her inside a well-known lingerie shop. The air was heavy with an overwhelming floral scent. Rows upon rows of intimate apparel of every color and design lined the shelves, ranging from sexy to scandalous. The store was deserted, save for a female clerk.

"You need a couple of those, right?" He pointed to a red demi-cut bra hanging in a corner. "Go ahead. Try that on. Try on the purple one, too. That looks good."

Whatever opposition she would have put forward withered under the hot, frankly sexual light in his dark eyes. A flutter of answering desire sprang up deep within her pussy. Swallowing thickly, she took the colors he wanted in her size, along with their matching panties, and strode into the fitting room, slipping into the very last room. The hot flash of promise in his eyes affected her just as much as if he'd touched her. Her hands shook as she struggled to unfasten her jeans and push them down her hips. She'd just placed them on top of the cushioned bench when there was a knock at the door. Cautiously opening the door, her eyes widened when she saw Nick on the other side.

She felt breathless. "What are you doing here?"

Nick stepped through the door, closing it behind him. The lock clicked loudly into place. Paige was forced to take a step back. Her pulse skittered. His eyes were dark and hot. She shivered.

"I don't think you should be here." Her voice came out husky and breathy.

His sheer size made the already small fitting room shrink even further. He advanced toward her, his lips tight with purpose. He wanted her, *now*. She put out a hand to stop him. "Nick."

The breath rushed out of her lungs as he pulled her against him. He dealt with her shirt with startling efficiency, pulling it off her in one smooth movement. His nostrils flared as he bared her to his gaze.

From the first look, Paige knew where this was headed. Sex between them was a foregone conclusion, whether it happened now or later. "The clerk will know what we're doing in here," she offered half-heartedly, already tipping her face up to meet his.

"Shh. I slipped in when she wasn't looking. Now you have to be real quiet or we'll get caught," he muttered outrageously before swooping down with a hungry kiss that she felt all the way to her toes. Her pulse thudded, and soon she was oblivious to her surroundings. She no longer cared where they were. It didn't matter that they were in a tiny fitting room of a lingerie store. It didn't matter that the clerk could come in any minute and discover them. None of that mattered. All that mattered was the overwhelming need driving both of them.

Nick hitched her leg around his waist, placing his jeans-covered cock directly against her pussy. He backed her against the wall and with a firm tug, ripped her panties in half. She uttered a choked sound of disbelief.

"I'll buy you another pair." He fumbled with the button of his jeans, exhaling a harsh breath of impatience, before managing to unfasten it and push his zipper down in one hurried movement. He wrapped her legs around his waist and in one smooth thrust, slid home.

Paige whimpered in pleasure.

"Shh," he whispered. He began to thrust in and out, with long, mind-destroying strokes of his hips. She felt deliciously wicked having sex in a fitting room. Scandalous. Forbidden. *Irresistible,* her mind argued back. How could she say no to the molten lust coursing through her bloodstream? She couldn't. So here she was, riding Nick Santorelli, biting her lips to control her moans, as he fucked her out of her mind.

Paige nuzzled his throat, her arms snaking around his neck. She could only concentrate on the thick cock that was plumbing her pussy. It felt so good. He knew exactly how to fuck her, knew when she needed it hard and fast, filling her all the way to her womb. His big hands gripped her buttocks, almost bruising in their tightness. His legs were braced apart on the floor, steady under their combined weight. He was so strong.

Swallowing the moans of pleasure struggling to surface, Paige shuddered in helpless abandon. She bit down on her lip to stem the scream that hovered on the surface. Nick nudged her lips toward his and swept in. His thrusts grew heavier, faster, and deeper. Each one drove the breath from her lungs, leaving her fighting for air. Reality dimmed, until it was only her and Nick in the world. Nothing else mattered except this.

When it came, her orgasm hit her hard. She stiffened at the onslaught of pleasure before shuddering violently. Seconds later, he followed her over the edge. Her hold on his sweat-slicked shoulders slackened, until her arms fell limply to her sides. He eased her down his body with a gentleness that was so at odds with the way he had just taken her. Her knees threatened to buckle, and it took her a moment to be steady on her feet.

"We really shouldn't have done that." Her voice was replete with satisfaction, and her words didn't have the effect she intended.

He grinned. "Didn't hear you complaining earlier," he teased. With surprising efficiency, he buttoned up his jeans and straightened his clothing. On the way out, he grabbed the lingerie that still hung on the wall. "I'll take care of these. You okay?"

"Yes." She'll never be the same again. When he left, Paige leaned weakly against the door. A small smile touched her lips. Paige liked doing something so spontaneous, so uncontrolled. She liked being naughty. A soft blush stained her cheeks as she pulled on her clothes. She'll never look at a fitting room the same way again.

When she emerged, the salesperson looked at her with a small, knowing smile. *She knows exactly what Nick and I just did in there.* Lowering her gaze self-consciously, she uttered a strangled thank-you before hurrying out of the store. She and Nick looked at each other and laughed like kids. He laced his fingers through hers. A warm, happy feeling filled Paige.

Chapter Eight

The night sky was clear and cloudless. Soft music swirled around them as they sat in the living room. A gentle breeze stirred the air through the open patio doors, carrying the scent of salt and ocean. Nick sat across from her, examining the Scrabble board laid out on the coffee table. "Hmm," he mused out loud. "What can I do with a z, r and s?"

Paige tried, but just couldn't suppress her giggle. "This could be interesting to watch."

He shot her a mock glare. "No fair. You're winning with triple point words that I've never even heard of."

Paige was enjoying herself immensely. A relaxed and laid-back Nick was devastating to her senses. His easy smile and teasing demeanor was as potent as the heated looks she was now used to getting from him. Earlier, he'd shooed her out of the kitchen and announced he was making dinner, refusing her offer of help. The spaghetti was delicious, as was the garlic bread and red wine that accompanied it.

Even the apron he wore while he cooked made him look sexier somehow. He was obviously familiar with the kitchen, something his mother had no doubt instilled in him. He was also neat, cleaning up as he went. Would he never cease to amaze her?

The sweater he wore clung to his shoulders. Her gaze dropped to the muscular thighs encased in snug jeans. The material was stretched taut, outlining his impressive form. He was barefoot, his feet strong, lean, and perfectly formed. Her pulse quickened. She wanted to see him naked again. As she stared at him, a plan began to form in her mind.

Seduction.

Nick made her feel beautiful and sexy. Why not try out her newfound confidence and seduce him? Her lips curved. With a sultry smile, she began to undo the buttons that ran down the front of her shirt.

He stilled. "What are you doing?"

She paused, her finger fiddling with a button before undoing it. "It's awfully hot tonight." The soft material parted, giving him a glimpse of her breasts.

His gaze zeroed in on the mounds, barely covered by the sexy bra she wore.

She didn't stop until nearly all the buttons were unfastened. Nick sat straight and unmoving, enjoying the show. This gave her confidence to pull her shirt apart and let it fall down her arms. All she had on was a flimsy, low-cut lacy bra that barely covered her nipples.

A noticeable bulge appeared in the front of his jeans.

Enjoying herself immensely, she stood up and let the shirt fall to the floor. Nick was a captive audience, gazing at her in rapt fascination. She ran the tip of a finger around and around her belly button, shooting him a look from under her lashes.

The air turned steamy, the heat emanating from his gaze alone was enough to thicken the tension. His lips curved in a sensual half-smile, the glint in his dark eyes full of anticipation. He sat back, his pose deceptively casual.

"You don't mind, do you?" Her voice was breathless, husky. Paige realized she liked being a sexy, *confident* woman. The thrill of feminine power acted as an aphrodisiac. It was exhilarating to know that the naked lust shining in his eyes was for her and her alone.

His low chuckle ran over her like a caress. "Hell no, I don't mind. This is your show, Doc."

She unbuttoned her jeans. "Tell me, Nick. If I wanted to seduce you, what would I need to do?"

"You want a lesson in seduction?"

The tip of her tongue touched the corner of her lips. She wanted to kiss him so bad. "Tell me what makes a woman sexy to you."

His wide shoulders moved in a brief shrug. "Sexy is different for every man. There are no set rules on how to seduce a man. Sometimes subtle is just as effective as overdone."

The deep breath she took almost pushed her breasts out of the bra. He couldn't take his eyes off her. "You don't like a woman in a skimpy dress?"

He leaned back and propped a knee over the other. "I'm a man. I appreciate a woman's body just as much as the next one. But more than that, how a woman feels about herself makes her infinitely irresistible. I find confidence very sexy."

She sauntered behind the couch and gripped the back with her hands. "Interesting."

His eyes darkened. "Or it could be the curve of her hip, the dip of her back." Their eyes met. "Or it could be sexy lingerie."

Her zipper rasped loudly in the silent room as she pushed it down. With a sexy little shimmy she never thought she could do, Paige stepped out of her jeans. Only matching red bikini panties covered her as she stepped from behind the protection of the couch.

"*Definitely* sexy lingerie," he added in a voice that throbbed with anticipation.

She wandered closer, stopping a few feet away from him. "I want to learn how to seduce you, Nick."

His brief laughter was choked. "I think you're doing okay on your own."

"There *is* one thing I want to do." She slid close, kneeling between his spread knees. His clean, masculine scent was a drug to her senses. "Will you let me?"

"How can I say no?" The only sign of his mounting tension was his white-knuckled grip on the wicker armrests.

Paige felt his heat through the denim as she slid her palms up his thighs. Fiddling with the hem of his sweater, she slipped her splayed hands underneath, seeking warm skin. The breath hissed from between his lips at the touch.

She slowly pushed his sweater up. A muscle ticked in his jaw as he pulled the sweater over his head and carelessly tossed it aside.

"You're so beautiful," she murmured, staring in fascination at the smooth expanse of muscled chest.

"I'm just a man, Paige." He rubbed her arms, moving upward to trace the low-cut cup of her bra.

Paige felt her breasts swell, the tips almost popping out of their lacy confinement. She leaned forward and skimmed her lips over his skin, feeling the muscles bunch and flex.

Nick jerked back.

Not to be deterred, she followed. With the tip of her tongue, she traced his nipple. She could feel his thundering heartbeat, and hers echoed the same heavy rhythm. A moan slipped past her lips as she explored and tasted him.

He gripped her upper arms tightly. "Paige."

"I want to taste you," she whispered. Her breath feathered over his navel, and she felt his muscles contract. His cock was stiff and long, straining against his jeans. She fumbled with the button, excitement and anticipation making her clumsy and uncoordinated. At last the button slipped through, and the broad, mushroom tip of his cock appeared.

"Maybe you should let me do that," he offered in a strangled tone.

"No. Let me." Her voice was tight and aching. It was hard to get the zipper over the bulge, but she finally managed to ease it open. Nick raised his hips as she pushed his jeans and boxers down below his knees and pulled them off. They joined his sweater on the floor somewhere.

Paige leaned back on her haunches and just looked her fill. He was mouthwatering. His cock was taut, the bulbous head proud. A drop of moisture teetered on the tip. She swiped it with a finger and drew it into her mouth.

"Christ," he groaned. "Are you just gonna look all day, Paige?"

She couldn't help but smile at that. "Patience is a virtue, Detective."

"My virtue went out the window the moment you stripped me naked, Doc," he countered in a dry tone. He gestured to her bra. "Take that off."

She arched an eyebrow. "I thought this was my show."

"So it is," he agreed in a silky tone. "But you have to give me something in return. Come on, Paige. I want to see those gorgeous breasts."

Shooting him a sultry look under the sweep of her lashes, Paige reached behind her to unclasp her bra. The look in his eyes singed her, it was so full of heat. The bra fell away. Sitting up, she cupped her breasts and pulled at her nipples.

He uttered a pained sound. "You're killing me here, you know that, right?" He reached out to touch her.

Paige shook her head. "Uh-uh. No touching."

"Not even one?" he asked in a persuasive, tempting voice. "Come on. Just a quick one."

She rotated her palms over the distended tips. "Like this?"

He groaned. "Woman, you have no mercy."

Paige was enjoying herself immensely. Nick's arousal fed hers. Beads of sweat coated his skin. There was an air of barely leashed urgency that surrounded him. But she wasn't ready to give in to him yet. There was something she very much wanted to do first. Bending forward, she licked the head of his cock.

Nick gave a strangled gasp. His hips rose off the chair, pushing the rigid length of his cock close to her mouth. Emboldened, she fitted her lips over the wide head and slowly took more of his cock inside.

"Yes," Nick rasped, gripping the arms of the chair tightly. "God, baby, just like that."

She took more of his length, her lips stretched wide until she could take no more. His harsh indrawn breath was like music to her ears when she traced the heavy vein on the underside of his cock with her flattened tongue. She went back up, loving him with her lips, tongue, and gentle teeth.

Nick gathered her hair in one hand, holding it back from her face. "Take me deep, Paige. Your mouth is so hot and tight. I want to feel it surrounding my cock again."

Paige did as he asked, pulling him in and holding him there for as long as she could. Having Nick's cock in her mouth was incredibly sexy. She *wanted* to please him, wanted to hear his muted groans of pleasure and see him drown in ecstasy. With renewed vigor, she applied herself to loving him. She bobbed up and down, holding the base of his shaft in her fist.

"Let me feel that tongue," he bit out between gritted teeth.

She slid her tongue down his length, fluttering all over the ridged head and sucking lightly.

"Touch your breasts for me," he requested thickly.

She knew the sight of her touching herself turned him on. She began a sexy, massaging motion, observing his reaction closely. Pulling the head of his shaft between her lips, she licked around and around, sipping from the slit of his cock.

"No more teasing," he growled in a rough voice. "I need more, Paige."

Her lips curved before she took him deep, letting him go in slow degrees. "Like this?"

A dark flush covered his high cheekbones. "Oh, yeah."

Reality faded. All she could see, think and feel was Nick, and the hard length of cock she was currently enjoying. She sucked and kissed him with abandon, thoroughly giving herself over to an act that she'd previously thought she would never take pleasure in. Needing his touch, she placed his hands on her aching breasts, seeking some relief from the desire that was racing through her. He didn't miss a beat, curving his palms around the heavy mounds. Paige sat a little straighter, giving him easier access, gripping his thighs tightly.

With an abruptness that took away her remaining breath, Nick pulled her up and got rid of her red silk underwear in one move. Paige tumbled on top of him, her thighs straddling his.

He entered her smoothly, sheathing himself to the hilt. Somewhere between the first and second thrust, Paige was gasping for breath. By the third thrust, she was mindless. She tried to move faster, but his hands held her firmly, resisting her efforts.

"Nick," she implored, nearly insane. She wanted him deep in her, thrusting longer, faster.

"What is it?" he asked thickly. Paige knew he was as turned on as she was, but he was holding back. Lust was rushing hot and heavy through her body. With a frustrated sigh, her fingers dug into his shoulders as she ground herself against him. "I need more."

He sucked the soft skin at the base of her throat. "What do you need, Paige? Tell me."

Arrows of heat zinged through her nerve endings as he pulled her skin between his lips. "Fuck me harder," she demanded in a whisper.

"I didn't hear you," he replied. Nick skimmed the tops of her breasts. Coming closer but not quite, sucking her nipples.

"Harder, Nick."

He suddenly thrust up in her pussy, reaching deeper than he ever had before, driving the breath from her lungs. "Like this?"

Paige shuddered. "Oh God, *yes*."

What had begun as a game of seduction had turned into a game of possession, of mastery. Nick held her fulfillment in his hands, and she wasn't above asking for it. Every thrust of his hips brought spiraling waves of hot sensation digging into her pussy. Fastening her lips to his, she gave him an erotic kiss. His response was instantaneous. He kissed her back, hot and deep.

Nick slowed things down and held her steady. He rolled his hips, burrowing deeper. Her breath hitched and stuck in her throat. Her pussy throbbed, stretched to the limits, waiting to be fulfilled. Paige rubbed her aching breasts against the soft hairs on his chest, wanting relief from the desperate want rippling through her.

"Don't stop," she begged.

"Shh, I want to make it last." Looking into her eyes, he trailed a finger down the curve of a cheek and made a maddening swipe at the rosy aperture between.

Paige bucked, shocked.

"I want to be there, too." He pushed a finger into her mouth and rubbed it against her tongue, moistening it. In the next moment, she went a little crazy as he slid it down her back and gently slipped inside her anus to the first knuckle. "I want to fuck you here. Would you like that?"

Dazed by the wave of shocked pleasure she was experiencing, she could only look at him. Her mouth had gone slack as soon as his long finger penetrated her there, and she'd long ago lost her breath.

"I'll make sure you're ready for it when the time comes, Paige. I want to fill you until you can't take anymore." He slipped in and out of the tight opening, stretching her, getting her used to the feeling.

Erotic images of him fucking her ass filled her mind. Weakness suffused her and she could only cling to him.

"It's amazing once you try it." His forbidden words elicited such a heated response from her that goose bumps formed on her skin. "The little bit of pain magnifies the pleasure you'll feel. And when I fuck you, I'll make you scream and beg for more."

Paige was lost in the erotic spell he wove around her.

"Will you let me do that, Paige? Will you let me fuck your ass?"

"Yes, Nick. God yes," she whispered with helpless abandon. She would let him do anything to her. *Anything.*

"But I'll have to prepare you first. We'll get you a small anal plug to begin with, baby. Something to get you used to the feeling of having something in your ass." His arms tightened around her. His hips never stopped moving, thrusting in long, languorous strokes that drove her crazy. "You'll do it for me, won't you?"

She nodded blindly. "*Yesssss.*"

Nick began to thrust harder. No longer wanting to prolong the pleasure of fucking her, he was all business as he held her hips down. He gritted his teeth as he pistoned in and out of her sopping pussy. Paige was moaning mindlessly, carried along by the intense ride. The tingling started from her toes and traveled all the way to her back before she shattered into a million pieces.

Paige hung on to Nick as she got swept up in a wave of unbearable pleasure. Dimly, she heard Nick groan and felt the warm wash of his seed, the hot pulsing of his cock. His orgasm triggered another one of her own, and she trembled violently. Their sweat slicked bodies stuck damply together as she slumped against him.

He pushed her damp hair away from her cheek. His sigh was one of deep satisfaction. "Doc, you can seduce me anytime."

Chapter Nine

The sun was creeping onto the horizon when Paige decided to give up on getting more sleep. She'd woken up from a disturbing dream. In it, she could see the tearful face of her neighbor, Diana. Images of her lifeless body in the elevator flashed in her mind. Over and over, she heard the young woman's scream of terror rising up from the elevator shaft the moment she'd been attacked. A pang of grief hit her. Diana hadn't deserved to die that way. She'd been a sweet, friendly girl with a ready smile.

Hard on the heels of that grief was guilt. Diana would be alive today if the killer hadn't been after her. The thought tore at her insides. She'd tried hard these past couple of days not to think about what happened. But it was always there in the back of her mind. She suspected that Nick was attempting to keep her distracted by sex. And although that proved to be effective at times, it never fully exorcised the ghost of guilt that hung over her. A tight knot of fear closed around her heart. It could easily have been her killed in the elevator that night. Suddenly cold, she snuggled closer to Nick. His arm was a welcome, reassuring weight around her middle.

"What's wrong?" Nick's drowsy voice penetrated her thoughts.

"Nothing," she assured him though her voice was shaky. "Go back to sleep."

He stretched and yawned before pulling her into his arms. "I'm going to ask you again. What's wrong?"

His steady heartbeat was cathartic to her. "If we hadn't been followed home, Diana would still be alive today." The weight of her misery was echoed in her words and voice.

Long fingers curved under her chin, tipping her face up. "Don't blame yourself. Don't lose sight of the fact that the killer is the one at fault here. He's escalating. He's desperate to find you. And he's willing to kill anyone who gets in his way."

She turned away with a sigh. "Things might have been different if the state-of-the-art security system the building manager was talking about had already been installed."

Nick froze. "Security system?"

"All the tenants were given notice that a new digital security system was going to be installed." Nick had gone still. She frowned. "What is it?"

He sat up, the sheet falling to his hips. "I remember Cecilia mentioning something about a security system that was installed in her building, too."

"You think there's a connection?" When he didn't answer, she blurted out the next thought that occurred to her. "The woman that was killed in the mall parking lot, Stella Kramer. Do you know if she lived in a building that had the same kind of security system?"

Nick's glance was sharp, assessing. "It might be a good idea to find out."

She sat up eagerly. "Why don't we go and check it out?"

"*We* are not checking it out," he drawled.

""It's a hunch that might lead us to the killer," she pointed out in a reasonable tone. "It does us no good to hide away here."

He snorted. "I'm not hiding. I'm trying to keep your ass safe."

Paige gave him a challenging stare. "Then what are we still doing here?" His answer was a warning glare, but she returned it with a stubborn one of her own. "You told me it's the same man who killed your sister, Nick. Don't you see? This might be the break in the case we need."

"I can't risk you out in the open like that."

She lifted her chin. "You'll be with me the whole time. What can happen to me?" she reasoned, trying to tamp down on her exasperation. "It might be the only chance we have to crack this case open."

His lips curved in unwilling amusement. "You've been watching too many cop shows, Doc."

"I don't want to run forever, Nick. I don't want to look over my shoulder every time I go out. What's the harm in finding out if there's a connection to the three murders?"

Nick pulled out his cell phone, activated the speakerphone function and called the station, asking to be put through to Detective Hernandez. "Hernandez, it's Santorelli. I need you to check something in the mall murder file."

"Yeah?" Hernandez grunted. "What is it?"

"Check if the victim's apartment building had a new security system installed."

"Hang on. I've got the file right here." The sound of paper rustling could be heard over the phone. "Nah. It doesn't say anything like that here." Hernandez paused. "What are you thinking, Santorelli?

"I know for a fact that my sister's building had just had a new system installed. Maybe that's the connection between the two cases. Maybe the mall victim's apartment had one installed too."

"You're thinking an alarm guy is our perp?" Hernandez asked.

"It's a hunch."

"I'll check it out. I've got your sister's file here and I'll look it over. Then I'll swing by her old building."

"I'm coming back up," Nick suddenly said. "Wait for me, will ya?"

"Fuck, Santorelli. Shit's gonna hit the fan when Captain sees you back here," Hernandez complained. "What the hell's the matter with you? Do you just like pissing off Ridgeway? You're gonna get your ass fired this time, for sure."

Paige saw the determination in Nick's face. Her heart went out to him, wanting to soothe the guilt she knew he felt, yet not knowing how.

"He can fire me after I find my sister's killer." Nick disconnected the call and turned to Paige. "I'm leaving you at the station while I check the apartment. You'll be safe there."

"You might lose your job," she cautioned him softly.

He shrugged. "I can find another one. I think I'd be a pretty good private investigator," he offered with a crooked smile before turning somber again. "I need to solve my sister's murder, Paige."

She knew it was eating away at him, being this far away from the action, from the possibility of finding Cecilia's killer. She would have done anything to take away the look of tormented guilt written on his face. "I'm sure Ridgeway won't fire you. And I'll be fine at the police station."

"You stay there and wait for me. So help me, Paige, if you even set one foot outside the station, I'll spank your ass until you can't sit for a week. Do you hear me?"

Paige gave him a teasing smile. "Your obsession is showing again. First it's my breasts, now it's my ass."

He gave her a stern look. "I'm not kidding around."

She hugged him. "I promise. I'll do whatever you tell me to do." She dropped a light kiss on his lips. "Anything."

He gave her a light tap on her ass. "Don't try to distract me."

She nuzzled the sensitive spot below his ear. "Is it working?"

Tightening his arms around her, he tumbled them back on the bed. "Maybe I'll just fuck you until you can't walk. That way I know you'll stay out of trouble." He rubbed his cock against her mound.

"No fair," she complained on an indrawn breath.

Their groans were simultaneous as he slipped inside her. It was quick, hot, and tumultuous. Nick fucked her like a starving man. She wrapped her legs around him and hung on. It wasn't long before they came together. A satisfied smile curved her lips. Boneless and weak, Paige felt too languorous to move. Nick eventually stirred and got up to take a shower. She joined him soon after, eager to get on the road and find the clues to the identity of the killer.

*****

Captain Ridgeway wasn't happy when he saw Nick and Paige at the station. "What the hell are you doing here, Santorelli? I thought you were keeping her out of sight."

Nick closed the door to the captain's office. "I need to check out a new lead."

"A new lead?" Ridgeway barked. "Your assignment is to watch the doctor, Santorelli. Not chase down leads."

"It's important, Captain." Briefly, he told the captain about the security systems installed before the women were brutally murdered. "I think it's connected somehow."

Ridgeway sighed gruffly. "Fine. I'll have someone check it out."

"I want to do it, Cap."

"Santorelli— "

"You know it's the same man who killed my sister, Cecilia," he stated in a quiet tone. "I'd like to go. Paige can wait here for me."

"You're too close to this. You need to let somebody else handle it."

"I'm just going to check it out. Let me do this, Cap," he said seriously.

The captain stared at him for a few moments before giving in grudgingly. "Shit. You always were a pain in the ass, Santorelli."

Nick knew Ridgeway was softening. "I'll go with Hernandez. He's up to speed on the case."

"Fine. I'll keep an eye on the Doctor."

Nick nodded. "Thanks, Captain. I really appreciate it."

"Get outta here," Ridgeway muttered.

Paige sat right outside the Captain's office. Nick squatted in front of her. "I'm going to check it out. I'll be back for you. I want you to stay right here and wait for me."

"I will."

"I mean it, Paige. The last thing I need is to worry about you. Stay here at the station until I come back."

"I promise," Paige reassured him softly. "I know how important this is to you." She curved her hand around his jaw. "Be careful."

Nick wished he could pull her into his arms and kiss her, but he knew that would only set tongues wagging. He squeezed her hand and stood up, gesturing to Hernandez that he was ready to leave.

While Hernandez drove, he pumped the seasoned detective for the latest development. His heart tripped as they pulled up outside the apartment building located a couple of miles from the local university. The hallway was brightly lit, though deserted. Loud blaring music could be heard from somewhere above, and the smell of food cooking wafted in the air. The apartment building's manager hovered behind him. "Look, Detective. I've had enough problems here since the murder. I don't want any more headaches."

"We're just here to ask some questions and look around," Hernandez assured the manager calmly. "If you want, you can stick around."

Nick rapped on the door of apartment 3-A.

A young man opened the door. "Yeah?"

Nick pulled out his badge. "LAPD. Mind if we take a look inside?"

The young man's gaze turned wary. "What for?" he asked, looking at Nick and Hernandez, then to the manager.

"It's regarding an incident that occurred in this apartment," Nick answered in a polite, patient tone.

"What incident?" he asked, suspicious. "I just moved in here last year."

"The incident occurred before you moved in," Hernandez spoke up. "A woman was murdered in here and our investigation is still ongoing."

Obviously taken aback by that revelation, the young man took a step back and opened the door. He led them to the small living room. "A woman was murdered in here?" he repeated, his tone a little nervous.

Nick didn't budge, his gaze rooted to a spot in the corner. That was where Cecilia's body had been found, sprawled in a pool of her own blood. He inhaled deeply, seeing the image vividly in his mind.

"Hey, dude, you're creeping me out. What the hell is going on?"

"Has anything out of the ordinary happened since you moved in here?" Hernandez asked.

"What's unusual?" The young man's thin shoulders shrugged under his faded blue shirt. "This place is pretty quiet. Tenants are okay, I guess. Haven't had any problems with anybody. And they have pretty good security," he finished, jamming his hands into the pockets of his frayed jeans.

"Security as in an alarm system?" Nick's tone was sharp.

"We take the safety of our tenants seriously," the manager informed him archly. "Every unit has an alarm system connected to a central control."

"Yeah, in fact, an alarm technician was here, oh, right after I moved in to make sure everything was okay." The young man glanced at the manager. "He said you authorized it."

The manager frowned. "I don't recall scheduling that."

Nick felt excitement curl around his stomach. This might be the clue they were after. But his face remained impassive as he spoke, "Would you mind if I check the system? I just want to look at the wiring and the connections."

"I guess it's all right," the young man replied. "The alarm box is inside the closet."

"Please don't break anything," the manager said.

Hernandez trudged behind Nick, peering over his shoulder at the small walk-in closet. Nick pushed aside the clothes and found the control box. It seemed innocuous enough, nothing out of the ordinary, until Nick discovered some wires protruding from behind the box cover. The wires disappeared through two tiny holes drilled in the ceiling.

He walked back in the bedroom and pulled a chair inside the cramped closet. Balancing precariously on the rickety chair, he lifted the vent. "There's a camera here."

Hernandez whistled under his breath. "Damn. You think that's how he was able to stalk his victims?"

"A camera?" The young man suddenly appeared behind Hernandez. "What the hell for? Is that thing recording?"

After a few moments, Nick shook his head. "It looks like it's been disconnected. There are some more wires up here. I'm going to check where they lead. I have a feeling they're connected to another camera looking into the bedroom."

He proved his suspicions correct later when he found a small camera mounted on another vent pointed to the bed. He pulled down the wire and saw that it was disconnected. How long had the pervert been spying on Cecilia? His sister must have been terrified. Icy anger twisted inside him. The bastard was going to pay for this.

"Son of a bitch," the young man uttered in disgust. "You mean somebody's been watching me?"

This was a huge clue in the case. Nick examined the small camera. "I don't think anybody's been watching you. I'm willing to bet this was disconnected soon after the murder." He pinned the young man with a stare. "When did you say a technician came here last?"

Raking a hand through his hair, he focused his worried gaze on Nick. "About a year ago. He came and said the manager called him to check on the alarms. He looked legit, so I let him in."

"My guess is he came to make sure he disconnected the wiring in here," Hernandez piped in. "I don't know how the crime scene investigators overlooked the alarm system. But then again, they wouldn't have had any reason to suspect a security system."

The manager looked horrified. "I swear, Detectives. I had no idea about any cameras. All I signed off on was a security system, no surveillance or anything like that."

Nick grunted and punched some numbers on his cell phone. "Captain, this is Santorelli." He talked in a low voice, explaining the situation. When he ended the call, he turned to the young man. "In about twenty minutes, a team of crime scene investigators will be here to sweep again for prints and other evidence they might have missed the first time," he informed the worried young man.

"Yeah, whatever. This whole thing is pretty fucking scary, dude. I gotta make some phone calls." He picked up the phone and started punching in some numbers.

"The bastard watched everything my sister did, and she had no idea," Nick muttered in a low, angry voice. "She had no idea the sick son of a bitch was stalking her, watching her all day, all night. She was a helpless victim."

Hernandez tapped him on the shoulder. "We'll get him, Santorelli. Soon."

"I'm a fucking *cop*," he went on as if the other man hadn't spoken. "I should have checked up on her more often, should have done more to protect her." Bitterness laced his tone and his face was a mask of self-loathing.

"Don't blame yourself. It's not your fault."

His fists clenched. "It's been a year and a half since she was killed. I swear, I'm going to get this guy, no matter what happens. I have to do it for Cecilia."

"Don't let the guilt eat you up, man. We'll get him." Hernandez paused. "Listen, I'll make a phone call to Stella Kramer's building manager and find out if they had the same kind of system installed. I have a feeling we'll find the same thing."

*****

Stella Kramer's apartment was located in a fashionable area of the city. The manager was more than cooperative, readily unlocking the door. Nick left Hernandez and the middle-aged man talking in low voices by the doorway and walked into the apartment.

Inside, it was painted in warm beige tones and decorated with tasteful furniture. The walls were lined with framed certificates, a college diploma, and a couple of small oil paintings. Nick looked at the pictures of a smiling, vibrant Stella Kramer scattered throughout the apartment. She didn't deserve to die the way she had.

"You all right, man?" Hernandez asked.

Nick's gaze hardened. "I'm going to check inside her bedroom. We don't have time to waste." He tried to clear his head. But guilt was a heavy burden to carry, and Nick was carrying a big one. The bedroom was undisturbed, pristine, the bed neatly made, covered with a flowered bedspread. Candles were scattered throughout the room and there was a lingering smell of vanilla in the air. It seemed like the bedroom was still waiting for Stella to return. He pushed the maudlin thought away and watched Hernandez poke his head inside the closet.

"Anything?"

"There's wiring in here, too," Hernandez answered, his voice muffled. "I'm trying to see where it leads."

"I'll check around." He went back to the living room and wandered around. On the corner sat a monitor and printer, but no hard drive. That had been taken as evidence and was no doubt being thoroughly examined by the lab's technicians. No answering machine either. There was a bunch of mail on the table next to the door. Nick picked it up and looked through them.

The building manager approached him. "Uh, Detective? I have mail for her in my apartment. It was mistakenly delivered to the wrong mailbox and the tenant gave it to me. She didn't know what to do with it."

"What kind of mail?"

He shrugged. "I don't know. It's just a plain white envelope. I'll get it for you." He scurried out of the room and came back a few minutes later, out of breath. "Here it is."

Nick glanced at the envelope. It was simply addressed to Stella Kramer. The script was neat, almost feminine, and there was no return address. His instinct screamed that this letter was an important clue. Picking up a letter opener from the computer desk, he carefully slit it open.

You looked so lovely last night in your silk negligee. The red really sets off your skin. I can almost smell your exquisite scent. Tell me, what is that cream you like to smooth on your skin every night? I want to know. I'd like to buy it for you, to know that you're wearing my scent.

Bile rose in Nick's throat as he read on.

Don't make the mistake of disregarding this like you did the last one. I know you threw my other letters away or burned them in the fireplace. You can't ignore me, Stella. I'll make sure *you don't ignore me.*

Hernandez came out of the bedroom at that moment. "What's up?"

Nick showed him the letter, careful to only hold onto one corner of the paper.

"Sick bastard," Hernandez muttered under his breath.

"He stalked her and terrorized her before he killed her."

"The whole apartment's rigged with mini high-tech cameras all around," Hernandez revealed with disgust. "He obviously came back and disconnected everything. I found small cameras everywhere, including the bathroom. He's got the whole fucking place wired."

Nick turned to the manager who was still hovering behind them. "Has anybody stayed here since the murder?"

He shook his head. "Her sister is making arrangements to dispose of all her things. The family is devastated."

"Did they find anything on her computer?" Nick asked Hernandez.

"Nothing. There were a couple of weird messages on the answering machine, heavy breathing and stuff. Other than that, they haven't found anything."

Nick trained his gaze on the nervous manager. "The alarm company that installed your system, was it High Tech Alarm?" When the manager nodded, his suspicions were confirmed. "It's the same alarm company. Come on, Hernandez, let's go check out the address."

Chapter Ten

As Nick had suspected, the address of the "alarm company" was bogus. It was a crumbling condemned building on the seedy side of town. He pushed aside a loose board covering the entrance and stepped inside. Dust motes flew about the musty interior. He pulled out a small flashlight. There were no signs of recent occupation, except for some empty candy wrappers.

"Nothing," he declared flatly as Hernandez brought up the rear.

"We'll find the owner of the building and see if there's a connection there somewhere," Hernandez said.

Nick's cell phone rang. It was Captain Ridgeway with some good news.

"We got a lead on our guy. Sanders and Ramirez canvassed electronics stores that sell high-tech surveillance equipment. They just got a warrant for the video surveillance in the store and invoices of recent sales."

He tensed, gripping his cell phone tightly. "Did they find anything?"

"The clerk remembers a man who looks like our perp, but he isn't sure. Listen, things could happen fast from here on out. Why don't you two come back to the station and wait here?" His tone brooked no argument.

Damn it. Frustration ate at him as Hernandez drove them back to the station. He clenched his fists with white-knuckled fury. He knew they were close. He could feel it in his bones. The bastard was not getting away this time.

Back at the station, he found Paige sitting in Ridgeway's office, leafing through a magazine. Her face lit up when she saw him. He gave her a wave and signaled her to wait while he talked to Captain Ridgeway.

"The warrant's on the way. Sanders and Ramirez will take the video and look at it. Hernandez—" he turned to the other detective, "—why don't you go with them and check out the invoices? Maybe we can get a hit on a name." He turned to Nick. "Why don't you get her out of here? Find someplace safe to stay. Keep under the radar."

Nick opened his mouth to protest but Ridgeway stopped him. "This isn't your assignment, Santorelli. Your duty is to watch over the doctor." With that, he was effectively dismissed.

After Ridgeway walked into his office, Hernandez tapped Nick on the shoulder. "I'll give you a heads-up when we have something."

He nodded gratefully. "Thanks, Hernandez. I appreciate it." He was just going to have to sit tight and wait for anything that might happen. Ridgeway was right. He had to keep Paige hidden in a place the killer wouldn't suspect. But he'd already learned his lesson. Just in case the station was being watched, he made plans to sneak Paige out without anybody being the wiser. He solicited the assistance of a female detective who drove them away from the station. Nick felt stupid, hunched down in the rear seat but he gave Paige a reassuring grin. After a safe distance, the detective pulled over and got out of the car, handing him the keys. In return, he gave her keys to the Jeep and made arrangements to switch later.

Nick decided to stay at the first motel he saw. He needed to stay close to the action, but he also needed to keep Paige safe.

He strode into the office and took care of registration before ushering Paige into their room. By the time he came back with their bags, she was already in the shower. Steam poured into the bedroom from the open bathroom door and he could just make out her shadow in the shower. He dropped on the bed and crossed his hands under his head.

The shower turned off. It wasn't too hard to imagine tiny droplets of water clinging to her skin. Right now she was probably slathering on moisturizer, the one with the scent he would always associate with her. She'd bend over and start with her legs, working her way up her thighs. He smiled. Then she'd massage some on her breasts, going around in circles before ending at her nipples.

Paige walked into the bedroom and caught his smile. "Something funny?"

His eyes caressed her soft dewy skin, pink and smooth from the hot shower. "I want to thank you for being a good girl today."

She grinned, obviously pleased. "Yeah?"

"Uh-huh. You were exactly where I left you. You didn't disobey me."

"I do know how to follow orders. Sometimes," she added in a teasing tone. "I think I deserve a reward."

His cock swelled under his jeans. He liked Paige like this, warm and funny, and barely dressed. He raked her body with his gaze. "A reward."

Paige tilted her head. "Definitely."

"What did you have in mind?" he drawled.

She eyed the thick length of his shaft. "Oh, I have several ideas, but they're all pretty much the same." Her voice had turned breathless and husky. Her tongue came out and moistened her lips.

"Well, we can't let a good deed go unrewarded, now can we?"

"Absolutely," she agreed silkily.

The temperature in the room rose several degrees. Every muscle in his body went on alert, excitement rippling through him. Any minute now his damn cock was going to push through his jeans. "Why don't you tell me what you want, Doc?"

"Well, now that you mention it—" she fingered the knot that held the towel together "—I do have a couple of things I wanted to try out with you. But I think tonight should be about what *you* want."

Nick swallowed as he eyed the precarious position of the towel. "This is getting more interesting by the second."

Her husky laugh raced over his sensitive skin. She gave him a look that was part innocent, part seductress. "What's your fantasy?"

He choked. Jesus, there were so many things he wanted to do with her. Where did he start? "Are you sure about this?"

"Oh, I'm sure," she murmured, holding his gaze. "Are you?"

He scooted to the edge of the bed. "I'm game." He pushed up from the bed and picked up the police-issued handcuffs from the dresser. He held them up for her to see. "You game?"

Her eyes darkened with heat. "You want to tie me up?"

"That and more, Paige," he answered huskily. "I want to tie you up and fuck you out of your mind."

It was her turn to visibly swallow.

Nick stilled. "Do you trust me?"

Her cheeks had turned a delightful shade of pink, but she scoffed at his statement. "I don't think there's even a question about that."

Nick tossed the handcuffs on the bed. The metal glinted dully under the white fluorescent lights. "It's up to you, Paige. We won't do anything you don't want to."

Paige untied the towel and let it fall to her feet. The implication sent hot waves of excitement through him.

"I'm ready when you are, Detective."

Pulling his shirt over his head, he dropped it on the chair next to the bed. He undid the top button of his jeans and pushed his zipper down. "Get on the bed."

She did as he asked, giving him tantalizing glimpses of her pussy as she moved. She sat back on her haunches and placed her hands on her thighs. Without knowing it, she'd assumed a position of submission. He inhaled harshly.

"Anytime you want me to stop, just say it," he instructed gruffly. Putting one knee on the bed, he knelt in front of her, his cock directly in line with her face. He almost came undone when she licked her lips hungrily.

Her gaze was glued on his jutting cock. "I understand."

He took his cock in his fisted hand and slid up and down in a languorous caress. Her moan reached his ears, the impact of the tortured sound lighting his every cell on fire. "Lie down."

The sheets rustled loudly in the silence of the room as she lay down on the bed. Her eyes were deep, dark pools of hot desire. She was perfect, with soft, yielding curves and satiny skin. His body screamed to just take her and fuck her until she begged for mercy, until pleasure overcame her senses. *No.* He had to get himself under control. He wanted to slow it down this time.

"Put your arms over your head," he ordered. "Hold onto the bars until I tell you to let go," he added, gesturing to the columns of the headboard.

"But I thought—" she murmured faintly as her gaze fell on the handcuffs. Arousal was written plainly in her face. She was so honest, so open and unafraid to show her feelings.

"Not yet, baby. I'll handcuff you a little bit later. Be patient."

Her breasts bobbed as she took a deep breath and nodded. Stiff nipples topped the generous mounds, the skin flushed a light pink to match her cheeks. She shifted restlessly under his gaze.

"Relax," he murmured softly. "This is about my fantasy, remember?" His eyes were drawn to the slight swell of her stomach. He traced it with a fingertip. "Do you know that I find this incredibly sexy, this little bump here?" He felt rather than saw her deep breath and mused out loud, "I don't know why women think it's sexy to be skin and bones. I like my women soft and full of curves."

"Nick," she murmured breathily.

"Now let go of the bars for a moment," he instructed. He flipped her over with a suddenness that obviously took her by surprise, judging by the little gasp that escaped her. He straddled her and slid his palms down her silken back.

Softly tracing the arched contours, he explored every inch he could reach. He dipped into the cute little dimples at the base of her spine. Giving in to the urge, he cupped the luscious cheeks of her buttocks and squeezed.

Her whimper was muffled by the pillow against her cheek.

He clenched and unclenched the plump curves, loving every wriggle of her ass. Pulling the cheeks apart, he swiped a finger down the puckered rim of her anus. Her loud, indrawn breath made him smile. Leaning forward, he licked her ear before nipping the soft fleshy part of her lobe gently.

"I could spend hours and hours playing with your ass," he breathed against her ear.

She moaned.

He turned her back over and their gazes met. Her deep green eyes were dazed and unfocused with lust. Nick fastened his lips to the base of her throat and sucked. "But first, I'll fuck your pussy until you beg me to stop."

Bending down, he captured her lips in a deep, tongue-tangling kiss. Her response was immediate. He delved deeper into her mouth until she was moaning in mindless abandon. He eased back from the kiss in slow degrees, pleased when she leaned up and tried to recapture his lips. "Uh-uh. Hold on to the headboard, Paige," he reminded her.

The protest died on her lips. With an unsatisfied huff, she settled back on the bed.

"Good." Nick took the handcuffs and wrapped it around her wrists, restraining her against the headboard. He grinned at the hot flush that spread over her face. Sliding lower, he cupped her breasts, concentrating on her delicious, plump nipples. He tugged until the tips were standing straight up, stiff and pouting. He pushed the luscious mounds together. A sharp stab of arousal hit him at the voluptuous sight. He bent low and fastened his lips to her tempting nipples.

"Ahhh," she gasped.

His hands tightened on her delicate skin. He swirled his tongue in patterns as he ventured lower. He smiled when her muscles contracted under his touch. Nuzzling the soft, downy skin of her lower belly, he inhaled deeply. The strong scent of her arousal reached his nose. He shouldered her legs wide apart. The first glimpse he got of her slick pussy was like a punch in the gut. The soft pink tissues glistened with moisture, the lips slick and inviting. He pushed them apart, exposing her clit. He gave her one long, luxurious lick from the bottom of her pussy to the top, his tongue rasping against the sensitive flesh.

Paige parted her legs further. "More."

In response, he pushed her legs high and wide. He fastened his lips to her stiff clitoris and sucked. Her scream sailed over his head but he didn't stop until she was twisting and bucking in his arms. He heard every panting, harsh breath she took.

He gritted his teeth and applied himself to the task of driving her insane with pleasure. His cock was painfully erect, the sensitive head dripping with pre-come. But he was determined to hold back. He ground his hips against the crisp sheets, trying to find a measure of relief from the ache torturing him.

"Nick," she moaned.

"Come for me, baby," he rasped against her clit. "Let me feel you come." He pulled her sensitive flesh into his mouth.

Paige stiffened and let out a scream. Her body bowed and contracted as strong tremors shook her. Nick held her tightly. He didn't stop pulling at her clit until she was limp as a rag doll. When her eyes finally opened, they were dazed and unfocused.

Drops of sweat fell from his face to her body. Watching her come always had the same effect on him. He loved that she felt such intense pleasure with him. His body shook with the effort to hold himself back, but he couldn't wait anymore. He had to fuck her now.

Surging on top of her, Nick took her face in his hands. "Are you ready for more?"

Still trembling from the aftershocks of her orgasm, Paige could barely nod her head. "Yes," she breathed. It was unbelievably erotic to be tied up like this, defenseless against his every assault on her vulnerable senses.

She whimpered as the broad head of his cock pushed inside her, forcing through the pliant tissues. He bent her knees until they rested against her chest, leaving her open and accessible. Sliding his fingers around her bent thighs, he sought and found her nipples. He pinched them gently as he pushed in to the hilt.

Her breath caught in the back of her throat. "Oh, God!"

He let out a strained chuckle. "I know."

Her hips rose off the bed, lodging him deeper into her. "Fuck me."

He pushed his cock in slowly and pulled out in small degrees.

She shook her head in protest, her damp hair sliding against her cheeks. "Faster," she gasped. Never had she felt more aroused, more helpless, than at that moment. She was ready to beg for more of the pleasure only he could give her.

He ignored her plea. His face was a tight mask of concentration as he surged in and out of her pussy. In. Out. Left. Right. Up. Down. Until there wasn't an inch of her sheath he left undiscovered and unexplored. He was driving her insane.

"Feel how well we fit, Paige," he bit out in a strained voice. His beautiful chocolate-colored eyes glittered hotly with lust. "I love it when your pussy clenches on my dick as if you can't bear to let me go." He slowly withdrew, his breath escaping harshly from between his lips. "Yeah, just like that."

Paige shivered and tightened her inner muscles. "Like this?"

"Again," he growled, his voice thickened by pleasure.

She complied, shuddering as her sensitive tissues clung to his cock.

Nick plunged his hands into her hair. "I can't hold back any longer." In one powerful stroke, he pushed into her all the way to the mouth of her womb, literally taking her breath away. He was a part of her. She was a part of him. No longer two separate entities, but one.

"Stay with me all the way," he commanded harshly.

Her eyes drifted closed. God, he was in so deep. His balls slapped rhythmically against her as he powered in and out of her sopping pussy. Like a man possessed, Nick took her with little gentleness. But she loved it, loved every forceful stroke, every little grunt of pleasure she wrung from him. He was fucking her like an animal and she wanted more of it. It felt so good…

Paige shuddered. Nick burrowed closer, his hips rolling and sinking, penetrating her deeply.

"Ohhhh," she moaned. Pleasure rolled through her in thick waves. The tingling started in her toes and worked its way up her spine. She was dizzy from the furious ride and could only hang onto the headboard.

"You feel so good. So hot and tight," he panted.

The feel of his skin rasping against her only added to the unbearable sensations flooding her. Her heartbeat thundered in her ears.

His handsome face twisted into a grimace of pent-up pleasure. "Come with me, Paige."

She lost all sense of time and place as she came. Dimly she heard Nick shout and felt the warm gush of his seed inside her. It went on and on, the long, hot orgasm rolling through her. Exhausted, she was only faintly aware of him unlocking the handcuffs and rubbing her wrists, bestowing a tender kiss upon them.

With a satiated smile, she shifted closer to him. Her eyes drooped and lassitude seeped into her bones. The last thing she saw before her eyes closed was the satisfied smile curving his lips.

Chapter Eleven

Paige drifted slowly awake a few hours later, the pealing of a cell phone penetrating the deep fog of sleep enshrouding her senses. Rubbing her eyes, she sat up just as Nick stretched out a long arm and grabbed the offending phone.

"Santorelli," he murmured drowsily. Seconds later, he jackknifed into a sitting position. "What's his name? You got an address? Where? When did this happen? Damn it, why didn't you call me before now?" He listened intently. "All right. I'm on my way." He flipped the phone closed and turned to her. "They tracked down his address. They've got him cornered inside his house. I'm going."

She didn't even hesitate. "Of course."

Nick was already pulling on his jeans and shirt. "They got him. They got a name and an address. Derek Anderson. He lives a few miles from here. I want to see the bastard, Paige. If he's alive, I want first crack at him." He looked at her with concern. "I don't want to leave you but— Will you be all right here?"

Paige nodded. Her heart ached for him. She understood his need to see this through. The guilt he'd been carrying around since his sister's death weighed heavily on him. "I'll be fine. If they've got the suspect cornered, then I'll be perfectly safe here. Go and do whatever it is you have to do."

He grabbed his keys. "Stay here. I don't know what time I'll be back. I'm going to leave my cell phone with you so I can get in touch with you." Nick leaned down and gave her a brief kiss. "I'll call you."

Paige stared at the door long after he left, her lips tingling from the brief contact with his. *Be careful.* With a sigh, she plopped back against the pillow and pulled the sheet over her. She hoped they'd get the suspect so this whole nightmare could be over. The thought stopped her short. Once they got the guy, there was no reason for Nick to stay with her. She felt a painful twinge inside. They'd never talked about what would happen once the killer was caught. Could what they have be called a relationship? Her stomach sank. She didn't know what they had. They'd been forced into a situation where they had to be together all day and all night. Sure, they were sexually attracted to each other and the sex was great. Last night when he'd tied her up…

She reined in her runaway thoughts and forced herself to analyze the situation. She was smart. She could think this through. There was one important question in her mind. Once the whole thing blew over and she didn't need a bodyguard, would he want to continue seeing her?

It was probably foolish to expect too much. After all, Nick had a life before he met her. The thought left her with a gnawing feeling of emptiness. But she had to be prepared for any eventuality, including the two of them going their separate ways. The time she'd spent with Nick had been incredible. She'd learned a lot about herself and discovered that she was far from frigid. She flushed. It had actually been embarrassingly easy for Nick to draw a wanton response from her every time. One touch and she'd go up in flames. One kiss and she was a goner. She thought of all the things she'd willingly done with him. The old Paige would have never dreamed of doing half the things she did. The new Paige was daring and adventurous in bed. *Or anywhere else Nick wanted to do it.*

She didn't want to lose Nick.

She was in love with him.

Paige froze. She loved Nick Santorelli.

She didn't know how it had happened, nor could she pinpoint the exact moment her feelings had changed. All she knew was that she loved him.

But what if he wasn't in love with her?

She rubbed the area over her heart. There was no way she'd settle for anything else. Paige wanted the same kind of love her parents had for each other. She took a deep, shaky breath. If Nick didn't love her, she'd just have to go on.

No matter how much it hurt.

* * * * *

Paige waited for Nick to call or come back, but he didn't do either. She fell into an uneasy sleep and woke up, but still no call from Nick. She chewed on her lip with worry. What was happening? Why hadn't he called? It was difficult to sit there and wait for him to return. With the killer likely in custody by now, there would be much to do to wrap up the case. He'd probably be gone for a while. Unable to just sit there and wait, she took a shower and got dressed. When Nick's cell phone rang, she eagerly answered it, thinking it was him. "Hello?"

"Dr. Harrington?"

Paige frowned. "Yes?"

"Detective Santorelli asked me to call you." The voice was polite and friendly. "He said to tell you everything is okay and they got the suspect. You don't have to stay holed up where you are."

"That's wonderful," she breathed.

"Yes, it is." He paused. "Where will you be? So I can pass on the information to Detective Santorelli."

Paige bit her lip. Nick had said he'd call her. Maybe he was too busy to pick up a phone and had asked another detective to call her. She hesitated for a moment, unsure of what to do. But if they already had their suspect in custody, then everything should be okay. She didn't have to stay here at the motel any longer. "Tell him I'll be at the hospital. Thank you for calling."

Paige called her father and informed him of the latest developments in the case. Since the murders had happened, she had begun to see her father in a new light. John Harrington was a tad overprotective, but she had no doubt that he loved her. He'd been a stern father, one who kept her focused on the goals he laid out for her. She realized now that he'd done it all out of love for her. It had taken a lot for him to let her go out into the world on her own, but he had. By the time she hung up, she felt like she'd just entered a new and better phase in her relationship with her father. She called for a taxi and settled in to wait, excited at the prospect of not needing to hide anymore. When the taxi came, she hurried out of the room, pulling the door closed behind her.

Nick's cell phone began to ring where Paige had left it on the table.

The taxi dropped her off at her apartment. She carefully circled the yellow tape that still cordoned off the elevator and walked up the four flights of stairs to her floor. She refused to think about the tragic events that had occurred here just a few days ago. Gathering up some essentials and her car keys, she paused by the door. The apartment didn't feel the same, she realized. With more than a touch of sadness, she realized she was going to have to look for a new place to live. It didn't feel like home anymore. It was time to heed her father's advice and get an apartment away from the city.

She drove to the hospital, feeling more at ease. The familiar antiseptic scent assailed her as soon as she walked through the automatic doors. The lobby was a busy hive of activity. Only now did she realize how much she'd missed it.

Dr. Meyer, County's Medical Director, approached her. "Dr. Harrington." He looked surprised to see her.

"Dr. Meyer," she returned the greeting with a smile.

"Am I to assume you're back?" he asked. "Everything's been resolved, I take it?"

She nodded. "I believe it has, or soon will be," she told the Medical Director. "They've got their suspect. I figured it was safe to come back to work. I wanted to check on a couple of my patients."

Dr. Meyer smiled. "That's the mark of a dedicated doctor. I know you've been through quite an ordeal. Maybe you should take it easy to begin with," he suggested. "Do your rounds, and maybe tomorrow we can work you back into the schedule."

"Thanks. I'm grateful for your understanding of the situation, Dr. Meyer," she added.

He waved his hand. "Yes, yes. Well, anything to ensure your safety." His beeper went off. "I'm being summoned. I'll see you later, Paige."

Paige strode to the bank of elevators. There was one patient she was particularly eager to see. Anna Wainwright was an eleven-year-old girl who had suffered tremendous trauma in a car accident. Through it all, the sweet little girl had been brave and heart-achingly positive. She wanted to check on her.

The skin on the back of her neck prickled. *Someone was watching her.*

With a frown, she turned around. People of all ages milled around the hospital lobby, along with nurses and various medical technicians. There was nothing out of the ordinary. Her glance swept the area. Nobody seemed to be looking at her. She was probably just being paranoid.

Stop it. There was no need to be scared now. The police had the killer at this very moment and there was no reason to think he could still be after her. Just the same, the feeling of being watched stayed with her through the short elevator ride. Relief swept through her when she stepped out onto the ICU unit on the fifth floor.

After a quick stop at the nurses' station where she perused Anna's chart, she made her way to the little girl's room. She peeked inside. Anna was still connected to a series of machines that continually monitored her vital signs. A bandage was wrapped around her head and she still looked pale. Her angelic face lit up when she saw Paige at the door.

"Dr. H!"

With a laugh, Paige walked into the room and sat next to her on the bed. "How are you feeling?"

Anna beamed. "I've been doing okay. But I'm going to be better now that you're back." She looked at Paige earnestly. "I missed you, Dr. H. Nobody can take care of me like you."

"I missed you too, Anna." She gently tucked the little girl's thin hair behind one ear. "Now, let me just do a quick check on you, okay? I want to make sure you're on your way to getting better so you can go home."

She'd just slipped the stethoscope on when the door opened. Expecting a nurse, the smile froze on her face when she saw that it was *him*. Derek Anderson, the killer. Her heart thudded against her chest. Fear skittered along her spine and she glanced quickly at Anna.

The little girl sensed that something was not right. She reached for Paige's hand. "Who is he, Dr. H?"

Anderson advanced into the room and gave them a nasty, evil smile. "Tell her who I am, Dr. Harrington."

Paige swallowed and strove not to show her fear when she stood up and faced him. "What do you want?"

"Isn't it obvious?" His voice rang with sarcasm. "You're my getaway ticket. With you as my hostage, the police won't have any choice but to let me go."

She shifted and covered Anna protectively. "Leave her out of this."

He cocked his head. "That is totally up to you. If you come with me without a fuss, I won't have to hurt her. Right, little girl?" he asked Anna, his tone patently false and sinister. "You don't want to die, do you?"

Her eyes full of fear, Anna squeezed Paige's hand. "Dr. H? Is he a bad man?"

Paige patted her little hand reassuringly. "Don't be scared." She infused her voice with a confidence she wasn't feeling. "Everything will be just fine." Her glance touched on the emergency button that rested a few inches from Anna's hand.

"I wouldn't do that if I were you," he warned in a menacing tone. "Even if you were able to press it, they'd be too late. I'll kill you and the girl first."

Paige lifted her chin. "What do you want?"

He smirked. "Just you, Doc. Come with me for a little ride down to the Mexican border. That sports car of yours should get us there in no time."

Fear twisted inside her, but she refused to let him see it. "It won't be that easy. There are too many people around here. Somebody's bound to notice."

His lips curled in an ugly sneer. "And if somebody does, I'll simply kill you and run away. I've gotten away with everything so far, one more body won't stop me."

She stared at him, thinking furiously about what she can do. First things first, she needed to get him away from Anna. She wouldn't allow anything to happen to the little girl.

He gestured to the door. "Shall we?"

Paige hesitated.

"I have a gun pointed at you under this jacket, Doctor." He drew back the leather jacket and brandished a small gun in his hand. "Try anything and you'll die."

She stepped away from the bed.

"Dr. H," Anna cried out, tears in her eyes.

"It's all right," Paige reassured her. "Don't worry."

"Don't even think of calling anybody, little girl," he warned. "If I even suspect anything's wrong, I'll kill your precious Dr. H. Do you understand?"

Anna nodded fearfully.

"Leave her out of this," Paige hissed.

He opened the door, holding her arm in a bruising grip. "Try anything and you're dead, do you hear me? Now, we'll walk out of here, nice and easy. We'll take the stairs down and go out into the parking lot. We'll get into your car and you'll drive us to the border. If you're good, I'll let you go." He stepped closer to her and sniffed her hair. "Or maybe I'll take you with me and have some fun."

Her skin crawled and she turned away in disgust. "You make me sick."

There was no doubt in her mind that he would rape and kill her when he had the chance. She had to escape and get to safety. But she had to get him away from Anna first.

He tightened his grip on her arm and smiled when she winced in pain. "You think you're too good for me, don't you? That's what the others thought, too. But in the end, they begged me for it." He pulled her roughly against him. "Just like you'll be begging me to fuck you, too."

Bile rose to her throat. "You're insane."

His sick laughter echoed inside the room. "They all said the same thing. But in the end, I got my way. They were powerless to stop me, just like you." He opened the door and glanced quickly outside. "Now remember, don't bring attention to yourself. One wrong move and you'll regret it. I'll kill you first," he warned, then indicated Anna with a tilt of his head. "Then I'll come back and finish her off."

He pushed her into the hallway and motioned toward the stairs. Gritting her teeth, Paige complied. Her thoughts were racing like mad. She had to think of a way to get away from him before they reached her car. By then it would be too late.

Oh Nick. Where are you? She hoped they'd discovered by now that the killer had eluded them. She stumbled as he pushed her down the steps.

"Hurry up," he hissed.

Paige said a quick prayer even as she hurried down the stairs to the first floor. She had to do something. But what could she do to get away from him?

*****

Nick ran out of the elevator and down to the nurses' station. Anger and fear were running rampant through his veins. Once he got a hold of Paige, he swore he was going to wring her neck. He'd told her, *told her* to stay at the motel and wait for him. He'd been furious when he'd returned to find Paige gone and his cell phone sitting on the table. Especially since the killer was still out there.

Trying to keep the panic from his voice, he asked if anybody had seen Paige. One of the nurses pointed to a room down the hall. Nick burst into the room, finding a little girl in tears. She jumped with fear upon seeing him.

"Where is she?" he asked. He went cold. Something was very wrong. "Where is Dr. Harrington?"

"A bad man took her."

His worst fear had come true. Striving for a calm tone, he swallowed the lump of fear lodged in his throat. "Where did they go?"

She wept. "I don't know. All he said was if she did anything, he was going to kill her. And I couldn't let anybody know because he told me not to, or he was going to hurt Dr. H. Please, help her."

"How long ago was this?"

"A-A few minutes ago," she replied shakily.

They were still here. "Call the nurse and tell her to call the police. Tell them what you told me." Without waiting for a response, Nick ran out of the room. He looked left and right. *Think, think.* Anderson wouldn't have taken the elevator with Paige. That was too risky. *The stairs.*

He barreled into the stairwell and took off at a dead run. He heard faint voices below and barely made out Paige's. Then he heard a door slam. Adrenaline rushed through his body. The bastard was not going to get out of here with Paige. Not while he was alive.

When he made it out to the parking lot, he spotted them immediately. They were headed for Paige's car. His chance of stopping them was slimmer once they got in the vehicle. He had to stop them right here and right now.

He drew to a stop a few feet away from them and pulled out his gun. "Stop right there."

Paige froze and gasped as the man walking behind her wrapped his arm around her neck and pivoted to face Nick.

Nick saw the fear in Paige's eyes. "Let her go, Anderson," he growled.

"You must think I'm stupid. The good doctor—" he tightened his hold on Paige's neck, "—will be my ticket out of here. How'd you like the fire I started, huh, Detective? And the body you found in my house?" He laughed. "I had you all running around in circles before you realized it wasn't me in there. You're all so easy to fool."

Nick kept his gun pointed steadily at him. "You're not going anywhere."

"You won't risk her life, will you?" Anderson sneered. "Her daddy won't like it." He pulled Paige closer to the Porsche. "That's why you're not going to stop us, Detective. We're going to get in her car and drive away from here."

Nick took a step closer. *Just a clear shot,* he thought. *One clear shot and he's dead.*

"And then maybe I'll fuck her, just like you did," Anderson drawled.

Gritting his teeth, Nick tried to meet Paige's gaze for a split second. *Try to get away from him. Move, Paige!* He didn't have a clear shot. Anderson was using Paige's body as a shield. *Fuck!*

"I'm looking forward to sampling the Doc's charms." He sniffed her hair. "I'm going to enjoy her. She smells real good. Maybe I'll keep her with me for a while for amusement."

Don't lose control. That's what he wants you to do. Nick kept his hand steady and his face expressionless.

Anderson's gaze hardened. "Lower your gun, Detective, or I swear I'll shoot her."

They were standing by her car. Nick knew it was now or never. He took a deep breath and began to let his hand drop slowly. "I'll come get you, Paige." He kept his face impassive but he desperately willed her to get his message somehow. "Remember what I told you in the car the other night. Just remember that."

Paige blinked.

Nick willed her to remember. *Goddammit, I need you to remember!*

Anderson looked at him then at Paige suspiciously. "Enough! Open the fucking door, Doctor." Roughly, he pulled Paige against him.

Paige suddenly went limp. Anderson yelped and tried to pull her back up. That small opening was all Nick needed. He pointed his gun and fired.

Anderson's eyes went wide with shock as he fell. Blood ran in rivulets down his face from the gaping hole on his forehead.

Paige screamed.

Nick ran to her and quickly pulled her behind him, prodding Anderson with his foot. The bastard was dead. Pulling her shaking body in his arms, he held her tight. Police cars with sirens blaring came screeching to a halt in the hospital parking lot.

"Why the hell didn't you stay in the motel like I told you to?" Nick demanded angrily. Now that the danger was over, his anger roared to the surface. He grabbed her arms and shook her. "How could you put yourself in danger like that? What if I hadn't gotten here in time? You could be halfway to anywhere by now. Or worse, he might have already killed you."

Paige was unable to speak, trembling violently, hurt shining in her eyes.

Nick knew he was being unreasonable, but he couldn't forget the fear he'd felt when he'd returned to the motel and found her gone. "Do you have any idea what Anderson could have done to you? Just once, couldn't you have followed my instructions?" he asked harshly.

"Nick, I'm sorry—"

He interrupted her with an angry slash of his hand. "You'd be sorry all right, if he had gotten away with you.

Because he would have raped you before he slit your fucking throat." He ignored her pale face and halted her explanation. "I don't want to hear it, Paige."

He ran his fingers through his hair, his hands shaking. He still wasn't completely calm. Fear had taken root in his heart and still hadn't let go. The thought of what that bastard Anderson could have done to her...well, he couldn't even bear to think about it. He swallowed. He'd never felt that way before. The utter helplessness that had taken over him was an alien feeling. It was unsettling and scary.

Out of the corner of his eye, he saw Captain Ridgeway heading toward him. "I have to wrap this up. I need to talk to Ridgeway."

He walked away without looking back. He knew he was hurting her, but he couldn't stop himself from walking away. His stride lengthened as he met up with the Captain. He needed a clear head to figure out what the hell was happening to him.

Chapter Twelve

Paige looked out the window of her brand-new apartment. The day was overcast and it was rather chilly, but the waves crashing onto the beach were a beautiful and calming sight. Her father had happily approved of the location and even oversaw the moving company that transported her furniture. She was slowly settling in. Little by little, the airy one-bedroom apartment by the beach was beginning to feel like home. The one dim part of her life was Nick. It had been a month since the shooting and he still hadn't called her.

With a frustrated sigh, she turned away from the view. *Why hadn't he called?* Did it mean their affair was over? Was that what they'd had? An affair? Her frustration mounted. She wished she was a sophisticated woman who could figure the difference between a relationship and a temporary affair. It was certainly more than that on her part. She was in love.

It was obvious he didn't feel the same way about her. A heavy weight settled on her chest. If he did, surely he would have called her by now. She pushed open the sliding glass doors and walked onto the deck. Pulling her sweater tighter around her, she stared at the rolling ocean waves. Maybe it *was* over. Maybe she should chalk it up to experience. Ignoring the twinge of pain in her heart at the thought, she breathed deeply. *No. I can't just give up.*

She glanced back at her reflection in the glass. Her windblown hair tumbled wildly down her back. She'd gotten rid of her eyeglasses permanently, in exchange for soft contact lenses. She wore hip-hugging jeans and a close-fitting sweater over her shirt. The woman who stared back at her bore no resemblance to the mousy, loose clothing-wearing Dr. Paige Harrington. Under Nick's tutelage, she'd blossomed into a sensual, confident woman.

A sensual, confident woman wouldn't just sit back and let her man go, would she? No. A sexy, confident woman would go out there, seduce the socks off her man and get him back. Her spine straightened. If she wanted Nick, she'd have to do something about it.

Seduce him. That's what she needed to do. She needed to drive him crazy with lust until he begged for mercy. *But what if he didn't want her back?* Paige refused to even consider that possibility. For the first time in her life, she was in love. The old Paige would have just accepted the status quo. The new Paige would grab the reins and do whatever she needed to do to get Nick back.

* * * * *

Nick sat with his feet propped up on the wrought iron table in his parents' backyard. He bounced a small tennis ball against the white railing surrounding the patio.

It's been a month since I last saw her. Thirty-one days, seven hours and twenty-five minutes to be exact.

He sighed and caught the ball neatly. One month since he'd left her in the hospital parking lot, looking stricken and hurt. He was such an insensitive fool. The sheer terror he'd felt upon seeing her with Anderson was something he'd never before experienced. The fear had almost paralyzed him. The thought of losing her was unbearable.

He'd never felt that way before about a woman.

Oh, he'd tried to forget her. He'd even tried to go out on a date. But for all the attention he paid the poor woman, she might as well have been dressed in a sack with a paper bag over her head. By the end of dinner, he'd had a rip-roaring headache and couldn't wait to go home. Apparently, she hadn't liked him either. When he pulled up in front of her building, she'd gotten out without a word and slammed the car door for good measure.

Grimacing at the memory, he threw the tennis ball harder and missed the railing. Anthony chose that moment to walk through the rear gate, and caught the ball as it went sailing over his head.

His brother shook his head as he stepped on the porch. "Still moping?"

Nick threw him a sour look. "I do *not* mope."

Anthony threw his head back and laughed. "Will you look at yourself? You've been sitting here all afternoon, feeling sorry for yourself. You're beginning to scare Mom."

Nick didn't bother to answer.

His brother sat down next to him. "I saw Paige yesterday. She came to my office for a briefing."

Nick sat up. "How is she?"

"She looks great," Anthony replied. A frown wrinkled his brow. "Why don't you just call her, bro?"

He slumped back on the chair. "It's not that easy."

"Boy, I never thought you were a wuss."

Nick stiffened. "Who're you calling a wuss?"

"Look, *so what* if you walked away and never called her? I'm sure she'd understand that you were scared shitless she was going to die. If you have to go down on your knees and beg her forgiveness, then do it."

Nick looked at his brother with surprise.

Anthony grinned. "Hey, I'm only trying to help." He clapped his brother on his back. "It's not easy being in love, huh?"

He winced. "I'm not sure what I'm feeling."

"I think the great Nick Santorelli has been tamed."

Was it true? Is that what'd been bugging him? He'd been moping around since the day he left her. He missed her laughter and missed her intelligent conversation. He missed holding her in his arms. He hadn't had a good night's sleep without her. Life just wasn't the same without her. *Damn.* He was one sorry fool.

His shoulders squared with determination as he stood up. He was going to see Paige and apologize, grovel if he had to. "I'll see you later. There's something I have to do," he murmured absently. If he'd looked back, he would have seen his brother grin and shake his head.

But just as he got into his car, his cell phone rang. It was Ridgeway. "I need you to check out a report of a burglary at this address."

Nick scrambled to grab a piece of paper and write down the address. "Cap, I'm going to need a couple of days off after this."

"Get this done then we'll talk. This is top priority, Santorelli," Ridgeway barked before hanging up.

Nick tossed the phone on the seat next to him and pulled out into traffic. He glanced at the address. It was going to take him at least twenty minutes to get there. He'd wrap this one up quick. Before the day was over, he was going to see Paige.

*****

Paige chewed on a nail and glanced at the wall clock for the umpteenth time. *Where was he?* She smoothed the shirt down her sides and reassured herself over and over. She could do this. She could seduce Nick.

The doorbell rang.

Paige jumped. Taking a deep breath, she moved deeper into the shadowed living room. The doorbell rang again, this time followed by a curt knock. She bit her lip. When the bell rang for the third time, followed by a loud thud on the door, she grinned. Hopefully he would get impatient enough to just come in.

"LAPD."

Her heart was thudding with nervousness. Resisting the urge to check her reflection in the mirror, she stood still. "Come in," she called. "The door's unlocked."

The knob turned and the door swung open slowly. Paige could see Nick standing at the doorway, his hand ready to draw the gun holstered to his side. He eased into the room carefully, checking his surroundings.

"Hello, Detective." She came out in the open slowly.

"Paige?" He frowned. "What the hell's going on?"

A delicate shrug lifted the hem of the long-sleeved shirt she wore higher, exposing her bare legs. "You didn't call, so I decided to take matters into my own hands."

His gaze was glued to her as she shifted closer to him. Paige stifled a grin as he took in the generous amount of cleavage exposed by the partially unbuttoned shirt, the long expanse of her legs, and her feet encased in strappy, red stiletto heels. When she bought them, the salesperson had assured her they were "fuck me" shoes. Judging by Nick's reaction, they were working.

Nick closed the door behind him and faced her. Arousal tightened his handsome features. "I'm sorry I haven't called you. Will you let me explain?" he asked, his hot gaze raking over her.

She crossed her legs as she sat perched on the arm of the couch and swung her foot lazily. Nick took this all in with hungry eyes. Paige shot him a sultry smile. "Maybe later, if you're a good boy."

Obvious relief was written on his face at her reaction. He grinned. "Oh, I'm very good," he murmured, his tone full of sexual promises.

Paige gestured for him to sit down. Nick positioned himself on the couch, stretching his long, muscular legs in front of him. His shirt was pulled taut across his chest, his arms stretched out on the back of the couch. His pose was deceptively casual, but the thick length of flesh pushing against his pants indicated that he was very much aroused.

Her confidence grew. She teetered on the ridiculously high heels to stand in front of him. "I have a surprise for you."

Nick didn't move, but Paige sensed a subtle change in him. It was as if every muscle went on alert, coiled and ready to spring. "You have to stay right where you are. You can't move."

He grinned, a thoroughly sexy, *I'm a bad boy* grin. "Scout's honor."

Her eyebrow rose. "I doubt you were ever a Boy Scout, Detective." She stood in front of him, her legs apart as she fiddled with a button on her shirt. "I want you to know that I thought long and hard about what I'm going to show you. In the end, I thought you would like it." She pushed the button through the loop slowly. "Are you ready?"

"Baby, I can hardly wait."

Paige grinned before undoing the next button, and then the next. "If you remember, you've shown a…an obsession if you will, with my breasts."

He flashed a quick, unrepentant smile. "Oh, yeah."

She held up a finger, warning him not to move. "With that in mind, I thought you'd like this." With excruciating slowness, she pulled the sides of the shirt apart and showed him her surprise.

Her nipples were pierced with gold hoops.

Nick's eyes widened and he sat forward for a closer look. "*Christ*."

She cupped a breast. The delicate gold hoop dangled from her erect nipple. "You like it?"

He choked. "Are you kidding me?"

Paige laughed delightedly. "I guess you do." Inserting her finger into the loop, she tugged on the hoop gently. "It feels sooo…good. I can't wait to feel your tongue here."

He almost shot off the couch. Paige warded him off with a hand. "Uh-uh. You promised to stay there."

"Cruel woman," he muttered. He couldn't tear his gaze off her pierced nipples and he was breathing noticeably faster. "Wait 'til I get my hands on you. Payback's a bitch, you know."

She chuckled. "I'm looking forward to it." She slipped yet another button through its hole, exposing her navel. "I felt so naughty afterwards that I said to myself, *why not do better*?"

He swallowed. "There's more?"

"Oh yes, there's more." Paige drew the sides of the shirt apart to expose her newly waxed pussy. She swiped a hand over her mound. "Look at that. Smooth as a baby's bottom."

His hips jerked on the couch. "Damn it, Paige!"

She tilted her head and looked at him innocently. "You like it?"

His eyes were full of hot promise. "Come here and I'll show you how much."

Paige laughed and shrugged off the shirt, letting it trail down to the floor. Naked except for her shoes, she was amazed that she felt no self-consciousness at all. The heat in Nick's eyes boosted her confidence. She loved playing the role of a seductress. Rubbing her thighs together, she could feel the moisture in her pussy. The sting of the nipple rings were a pleasant sensation that added to her arousal.

"Oh, but there's more." She propped a high-heeled foot on top of her coffee table. Nick couldn't look away. Good. The last surprise was the icing on a very sweet cake. Keeping her gaze trained on him, she pulled her slick labia apart and showed him…

Her pierced clit.

Nick had gone still. A light flush covered his sharp cheekbones, and his nostrils flared. He couldn't tear his gaze away from the gold bar piercing the hood of her clitoris. "When the hell did you do this?" he rasped.

"I saw a full-service salon that offered full bikini waxing and certain…piercings." Slipping a finger between her lips, she moistened it before sliding it downward and swirling it around and around her exposed clit. "I did it for you."

In a flash, he was out of the couch and holding her in his arms. With an urgency that was feverish, Paige pulled his shirt from his waistband and pushed it up and over his head. The heat emanating from his skin hit her in waves. She shivered as her flattened palms touched his chest, moaning at the delicious contact.

Nick wasn't idle either. He cupped her breasts and gently tugged on the rings. A streak of pain-pleasure swamped her body. Trembling, she fought to unfasten his jeans and whimpered when they didn't budge. With an impatient mutter, he pushed her hands away and unfastened them himself, pushing them down along with his shorts and kicking them away.

She couldn't stop her sigh of pleasure at finally having him naked. Grasping his cock in her hand, she began to caress him in a light up and down motion. The breath hissed from between his lips.

He backed her against the wall and dropped down to his knees, instantly fastening his lips to her pussy. Her knees buckled. He laved the hood piercing again and again, swirling the tip of his tongue over and around her clit. Paige bucked against him, and would have slid to the floor if not for his hands cupping her buttocks, holding her up. Torrents of pleasure tore through her. With a suddenness that took her breath, she came.

She shuddered violently as a wave of intense pleasure slammed into her. Tremors were still shaking her when he picked her up and deposited her on her knees on the couch. He knelt behind her, nudging her legs apart. She panted as she gripped the cushions, forced to lean forward with Nick crowding behind her. Her breasts bobbed and hung over the back of the couch.

His callused hands slid from her hips up to her breasts. Her breath caught in her throat as he pinched her nipples, his cock surging into her pussy in one smooth stroke.

"Oh, God," she gasped. She glanced back at him, only to have him capture her lips in a deep, forceful kiss.

He took her mouth and conquered it, never ceasing the vigorous movements of his hips as he fucked her without mercy. Paige tore her lips from his and moaned and begged—for what, she didn't know. All she could concentrate on was his cock plumbing her pussy thoroughly. He was in so deep that her breath hitched every time he hilted. She leaned back against him, helpless and caught in the firestorm.

He splayed his hands over the mound of her pussy and toyed with her clit, the sensitive flesh yielding to his touch. Paige realized she was going to come again. With a soft wail, she stiffened as she fell over the edge once more. Dimly, she was aware of Nick letting out a rough groan before she felt the warm gush of his seed splashing inside the walls of her pussy.

His arms went around her in a tight band, creating a strong, warm cocoon. He shifted and reclined on the couch, pulling her on top of him. His heart beat a strong and steady rhythm under her ear. It was sometime later before her pulse slowed down to normal.

Propping her chin on his chest, she was amused at the wholly satisfied look on his face. "Does this mean you approve?"

He grinned. "You're shameless. Absolutely shameless."

Her eyebrows arched. "I didn't hear you complaining earlier."

Nick chuckled. "I may be crazy, but I'm not stupid." He tucked her hair behind her ears. "You blew me away. When I saw the rings on your nipples, I almost lost it right there."

She laughed in delight. "I noticed."

His hand swept over her smooth pussy. "And this. I want you to keep it this way. It's so sexy."

"You prefer it this way?"

His eyes turned hot and molten. "Definitely. I love to see your pussy glisten when you're aroused, just like it did earlier when I stuck my tongue high up in there and—"

Paige placed a finger on his lips. "I get the picture."

He grinned but sobered a moment later. "I want to explain why I stayed away."

Paige bowed her head, unwilling to let him see the sudden pain in her eyes. "Is there somebody else?"

He tipped her chin up. "How can you even think that?"

"What was I supposed to think when you didn't call me for a whole month?" she countered.

Nick sighed and began to explain. "I was terrified that Anderson was going to kill you. I thought I was going to lose you that day. For a brief moment, I couldn't fire my gun because I didn't want to take the chance that I might hit you."

Paige buried her face in his neck.

"I had to think. I *needed* to think. I'd already made up my mind to see you when I got the call to come here." He looked at her curiously. "By the way, how did you manage to get Ridgeway to send me here?"

She grinned. "I just asked him to do me the favor. He didn't let me explain and told me it was none of his business but that he'd do it. Just this once, mind you, so he said I better get it done right, whatever I was planning." Her husky laughter was muffled by his warm skin. "I think Captain Ridgeway is a closet romantic."

His eyebrows shot up in disbelief. "Ridgeway? You've got to be kidding me."

Looking down at his handsome face, Paige was filled with tenderness. "I love you."

He didn't even hesitate. "I love you, too."

"I'm so happy."

Nick toyed with her hair. "Hmm. I'm going to have some pretty interesting things to tell our grandkids someday. Stories about how grandma seduced their gramps. You think they'd be shocked to know their grandma has pierced nipples?"

She glared at him. "You wouldn't dare."

He laughed. "What do you think the doctors at County Hospital will say when they find out that Dr. Paige Harrington is a wild woman with some very sexy piercings?"

"I'll deny everything," she declared.

"You're the only woman I know who can look prim and proper while naked as the day you were born," he observed with a grin. He nudged her pussy open with his erect cock, slipping inside the warm sheath.

She sighed in satisfaction.

Nick tugged her face up to his and eased his tongue into her mouth. Soon, they were lost once more in the passion that flared between them. Held securely in his arms like this, happiness bloomed inside her. Nick was her lover, her friend, her bodyguard.

She couldn't ask for more.

About the author:

Beverly Havlir writes her books surrounded by plush pink and white heart-shaped pillows and soft, sexy music playing in the background. She plots her stories dressed in sheer, silky lingerie while eating bonbons and sipping champagne.

Now for a dash of reality…

After running around doing totally unglamorous chores all day, Beverly writes at night when all is quiet and she is (at last!) alone. Exhaustion disappears as soon as she sits down in front of her computer, doing what she loves best: writing stories that bring women's fantasies to life.

Beverly welcomes mail from readers. You can write to her c/o Ellora's Cave Publishing at 1056 Home Avenue, Akron OH 44310-3502.

Why an electronic book?

We live in the Information Age—an exciting time in the history of human civilization in which technology rules supreme and continues to progress in leaps and bounds every minute of every hour of every day. For a multitude of reasons, more and more avid literary fans are opting to purchase e-books instead of paperbacks. The question to those not yet initiated to the world of electronic reading is simply: *why?*

1. *Price.* An electronic title at Ellora's Cave Publishing and Cerridwen Press runs anywhere from 40-75% less than the cover price of the exact same title in paperback format. Why? Cold mathematics. It is less expensive to publish an e-book than it is to publish a paperback, so the savings are passed along to the consumer.
2. *Space.* Running out of room to house your paperback books? That is one worry you will never have with electronic novels. For a low one-time cost, you can purchase a handheld computer designed specifically for e-reading purposes. Many e-readers are larger than the average handheld, giving you plenty of screen room. Better yet, hundreds of titles can be stored within your new library—a single microchip. (Please note that Ellora's Cave and Cerridwen Press does not endorse any specific brands. You can check our website at www.ellorascave.com or

www.cerridwenpress.com for customer recommendations we make available to new consumers.)

3. *Mobility.* Because your new library now consists of only a microchip, your entire cache of books can be taken with you wherever you go.
4. *Personal preferences are accounted for.* Are the words you are currently reading too small? Too large? Too...**ANNOYING**? Paperback books cannot be modified according to personal preferences, but e-books can.
5. *Instant gratification.* Is it the middle of the night and all the bookstores are closed? Are you tired of waiting days—sometimes weeks—for online and offline bookstores to ship the novels you bought? Ellora's Cave Publishing sells instantaneous downloads 24 hours a day, 7 days a week, 365 days a year. Our e-book delivery system is 100% automated, meaning your order is filled as soon as you pay for it.

Those are a few of the top reasons why electronic novels are displacing paperbacks for many an avid reader. As always, Ellora's Cave and Cerridwen Press welcomes your questions and comments. We invite you to email us at service@ellorascave.com, service@cerridwenpress.com or write to us directly at: 1056 Home Ave. Akron OH 44310-3502.

ELLORA'S CAVE
ROMANTICA PUBLISHING

Printed in the United Kingdom
by Lightning Source UK Ltd.
119210UK00001B/48